CYPHER
Chronicles of Rah

Scott Hopkins

Published in the United States by Chaotic Designs Publishing,

Printed in the United States.

ISBN: 9781951902025

ISBN-13: 978-1-951902-02-5

Original Cover art by

RockingBookCovers.com

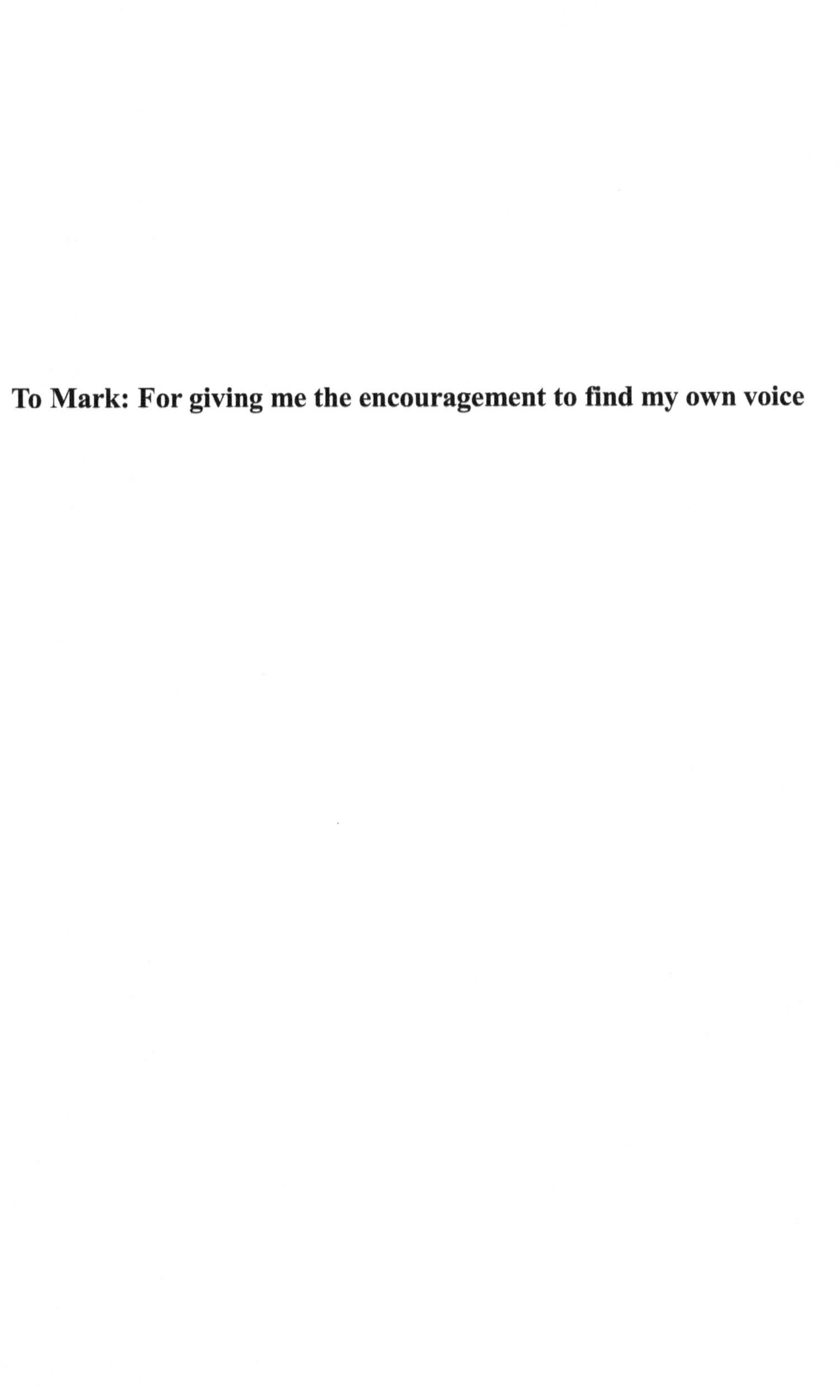

To Mark: For giving me the encouragement to find my own voice

ACT ONE

Well that's different! I normally wouldn't think anything about being in a dark room while trying to sneak in and steal corporate secrets, except in a situation where I didn't turn off the lights. That tends to make me pause and take stock of the moment. The darkness wasn't unwelcome, but it was a surprise, which meant I had to stand and let my eyes adjust to the subdued lights of the city outside the thick-paned windows. *This can't be good.* The lack of light in the hallway outside the office was also driving that knot in my gut to tighten as I fought the feeling that somehow I'd betrayed my presence. My ears and eyes focused on every little noise around me, searching for any sign I was in trouble.

As I moved through the office, with each step deliberate, the only noise that seemed out of place was a very dull oscillating thrum of vibrations in the air. The rather spartan décor of the office drew a smile as I thought about the rather buxom blonde executive who owned the office. When we met, she came across as a hard-charging female who had worked her way up the Megacorp ladder. Seeing her office, it dawned on me that individuals who tend to be rather aggressive like that don't need a lot of things. She had been very passionate, vivacious and hungry, and I had played on that to get what I needed from her. On some levels, I hated leaving her in this position, but business is business, and everything else was a means to an end.

I crept my way to the large white ferroplast desk sitting with her back towards the corner between panes of glass on either side. I couldn't help but smile again, thinking how the placement of the desk was perfect. It sat in a position of power in the room, with the backdrop of the city stretched out on either side of her, where she could intimidate even the hardiest client.

The oscillating thrum grew louder, holding my attention for a short second before I turned back to my quarry, the safe in her desk. The design of the desk seemed curious in that there were no obvious creases or edges. The sleek desk felt hard and smooth as I ran my fingers along the surface, looking for an imperfection or blemish. There wasn't any need to search the drawers or files. What I was looking for wouldn't be in a pencil cup or file folder. It was something that the company wanted very much, and had gone to a lot of time and trouble to get.

Gotcha! My finger ran across an imperfection: a plate along the inside edge of the desk, imperceptible to someone not searching for secret doors. With a light touch on the pad, a quiet click signaled victory. I smiled as a drawer at the bottom of the desk slid open, revealing a lighted keypad. I tapped the key code, which I had coaxed from my blonde executive, into the colored squares on the keypad. I was rewarded with a friendly hiss of electric gyros as the thin metal plate holding the key pad slid back into the drawer, revealing a clear crystal cube.

I stared for a moment at the perfect symmetry of the cube before sliding it out of its slot. I couldn't help but hold it up in front of my face, letting the lights from the city below refract through the lattice of circuitry inside the crystal. I admired the tranquility and beauty of such a development.

They called it Cypher, a DNA-locked organic data crystal formed from organic material and innovative technology, which harnessed more storage or processing power than any current computer system. It was no wonder the company wanted it acquired.

I needed to get it out of the building. As I admired the crystal, a random flash of light reflected across its face, a sweep of red light from under the door. I guess it doesn't pay to turn out the lights if I can see you coming, I thought to myself as I considered my options. I had to laugh at special tactics teams who failed to realize that technology they used as advantages tended to work against them with intelligent prey.

I slipped the cube into a felt pouch and dropped it into the pocket in my jacket as I looked around the room. One of the downsides of having such a minimalist décor in an office, I thought to myself. Nowhere to hide.

When I saw the second set of red lights sweep the hallway under the door, I figured it was time to come up with a good plan. I also realized that the oscillating thumping had grown even louder, vibrating along the glass.

My mind searched the sparse room; I spied a small black table sitting at the end of a long white couch near the large pane window. An idea came to me as I remembered that there was a secondary rooftop just a few feet below the office window. This had been what I was trying to avoid by coming in at night. I hated to use my ace in the hole so early in the evening.

My "ace in the hole" was a genetic modification developed to make me more successful as an operative: the slice and dice of Androken DNA and other chemical changes in my body gave me a few enhancements to make me a better spy. The most exciting being the ability to exude special pheromones that can alter a person's mood or perceptions. My control of these pheromones is acute, and I have learned, through years of training, to focus them and influence the emotions of others by doing so and even at times to erase myself from notice. It takes concentration to start and control in order for it to do what I want, and in the end it can be very poisonous to my body, but if used right, it could be very useful.

Realizing I had mere seconds before the soldiers busted into the room, I focused my thoughts on what I wanted to happen. My body began producing pheromones as I pushed the couch and the small table as hard as possible toward the window. The furniture slid across the smooth tile floor, smashing against the thick plate glass and broke through with a raucous crash. Almost on cue, three soldiers wearing black tactical gear and black goggles over their eyes hurried into the room. As they moved through the room, small automatic weapons were trained in front of them, their piercing red lasers sweeping back and forth as they moved.

I had to move careful, the pheromones radiating out from my body would distort their perception, but the range would be limited. I used the darkness to enhance the distortion they perceived. Sudden movements created shadows that would cause them to look harder. If I did it right, the pheromones fooled the soldier's minds into believing I wasn't there and I could walk right past them without them seeing me. Two of the soldiers moved straight for the hole in the broken window. The third moved toward the desk, checking the empty safe and looking for clues.

"Pickup One, this is Lead." The voice from the trooper in command filled the room. "Subject has dropped to secondary roof on west side of complex. No visual, need eyes on."

The two men at the window searched the roof below for signs of life. The third man drew very close to where I was moving along the long glass window; to my chagrin, his attention was on the desk and not on the "empty" room.

After what seemed an eternity, I reached the door. Looking back, I realized the thumping vibration in the air was an airship approaching the building. The craft hovered along the outside of the building, a bright searchlight pushing the darkness away.

I smiled as I realized the three men were more focused on the window than on the possibility that their quarry was sneaking out the door. I ducked into the hall, reached the stairwell and descended the stairs, keeping my ears open for the possibility of pursuit or someone coming up the stairs.

After making it down three flights, violent shudders shook the building and almost threw me down a flight of stairs. I held on tight to the rail as I looked up through the shaft toward the source of the blast. Darkness overwhelmed the stairwell as the lighting flashed out. Emergency lights flickered to life, filling the stairwell with an eerie white light that illuminated the heavy dust and smoke.

The look of shock on my face would have scared the most hardened operative, had there been anyone in the stairwell with me. Are they launching rockets at the building to flush out an invisible thief? I wondered as I continued my descent.

Whatever caused the building to shake threw the company's personnel into a throng of chaos as scientists and executives scurried to escape the building, while security and damage control personnel fought to get into the building.

The chaos in the lobby worked to my advantage, allowing me to slip out of the building by blending into the crowd. Fire teams and security personnel set up a perimeter around the building to push people back, but failed to corral the building personnel. I couldn't help but smile as I slipped into the night, the sirens and flashing lights creating a kaleidoscope of sound and color on the surrounding buildings.

Debris and ash drifted through the sky from the top of the building, a burning ruin of mangled metal sat in the middle of the street inches from the edge of the building's shattered office windows. I looked up and with a gasp, I realized the floor of the building I had been on and everything within about five hundred feet was gone. Missing. Destroyed.

My only reaction was a sigh of relief at the realization that the floor below the office had been a reinforced research lab, which contained the blast and kept it from sweeping through the stairwell.

I took a moment to thank my lucky stars that things turned out the way they did, then I faded into the crowd, with my unremarkable features working in my favor. I walked for a time, taking the opportunity to process what had happened and how things had gone so awry. My walk was aimless for the most part, carrying me far enough away from the building and hopefully random enough that I hadn't been followed. When I looked up, I found myself down the street from a local netrunner interweb café. I needed to rest and coordinate a drop for the item, but my mind was racing at how the plan had been literally blown to bits.

****

One of the advantages of being an operative in my business is the cool gadgets they give you. I pulled a small crystal from my pocket and slid it into the associated port. The clear crystal screen flickered to life at the base of the console as holographic representations formed above. Manipulating the floating icons with my fingers, I logged onto the interweb, then the crystal automatically directing me to the necessary website for the communication I needed to make.

To the outside observer, the site looked like a forum in which users could meet people for all manner of things or sell items. I found the appropriate page related to my missions: "Lonely souls looking for it all." The company used it to contact my handler for missions, and he used it to send me the details in an encrypted thread. I scrolled to the bottom and began my reply to let them know the job was done.

Crystal Goddess: Stopped for a bite in the Relard District. Found what I was looking for but got more than I needed. Hope you like shiny things. At our usual spot tomorrow, you bring the wine and I'll bring the glasses. - Blackknight

I read back over the language before I posted the message. It wasn't a perfect way of sending messages, but it was clandestine enough that no one would expect anything. During missions, the responses tended to be relatively quick, since my handler stood by and watched for trouble. There was no reason for me to suspect this mission would be any different, so I leaned back against the ferro-plastic chair and rubbed my eyes as I waited for a response.

My first order of business as I waited was medicine, Promium to be more specific. A medicine designed by RendarCorp to counter a number of blood-borne illnesses, including the side-effects of my talents. While mixing my DNA with Androken DNA brought about a number of useful abilities, and while these abilities allowed me to influence emotions and perceptions through an acute control of an advanced form of pheromones, increase my sense of curiosity and give me an intense awareness of my surroundings, my enhancements also created a side effect that could kill me if I wasn't careful.

The genetic splicing managed to create a constant battle inside my body, much like trying to give a human a blood transfusion from an Androken. While Androkens may look humanoid and genetic markers similar to humans, they are most definitely feline in nature. Just as a blood transfusion between a human and a cat would not normally work, daily injections of Promium were necessary to diffuse the immune reaction of my blood. What starts out as relatively minor symptoms – dizziness, tiredness and disorientation – tends to spiral pretty quickly into more life-threatening symptoms like septic shock and death if not treated.

The limiting aspect of my talent was that as I used it, the level of reaction increased exponentially. Promium kept the toxic levels in my blood from rising too high. While I'm certain that the company created dependence to this drug as a means to control their operatives, that didn't change the fact that I still needed to have a supply close by or I would die.

I pulled the small cylindrical auto-injector from my coat pocket and pressed the tip deep into my inner thigh. There were many places on my body I could inject Promium, but directly into one of the major arteries tended to speed up the process considerably.

I sighed as I felt the injection spread through my body. The weakness and fog in my mind slowly subsided. I had to admit, I was starting to feel rather old for my age as the adrenaline of the evening wore down and the Promium reset my body. I'd been running espionage missions for almost ten years, and this was the closest I'd come to being caught. One would think the life of a corporate spy would be all parties and alluring women.

That assumption, though flawed on many levels was not completely wrong. While my looks and size tended to make me unremarkable to most being someone who people tended to forget easily had become a great asset when stealing secrets for my employers. I had been too small to join the Republic as a soldier, and I didn't have the political connections to be in the Republic Intelligence Corps. Thankfully, the right looks, along with the right DNA, meant that the glamorous life of a freelance spy was in the cards for me.

In this world where Megacorps and governments controlled everything and stealing your competition's secrets was a form of politics, a nameless, faceless agent could be a valuable asset, working behind the scenes to drive policy and advancements over rival corps.

Lost deep in my memories over the last ten years, and letting the Promium do it's work, I realized that almost an hour had passed. I checked the activity logs using the software on my crystal. Still no response from anyone, which was a bit puzzling. The meeting time and location had already been set; the message was really just a way to let my handler know to coordinate the drop. While a delay in responding was odd, it wasn't unheard of, so I logged off, making sure the software on the crystal wiped any evidence of my activity. I figured after a long eventful evening, I should get some sleep before the drop.

****

Buoyed by the belief that I had a solid plan despite my current circumstances, I checked the area outside the building before heading down a street to the east and the nearest light rail station. Keeping a rather low profile, I moved along the streets, my senses and instincts hyperactively watching my surroundings as I tried to maintain a casual pace. I'd found out a few years ago that a hurried pace on a deserted city street in the middle of the night tended to highlight you, not hide you.

I reached the light rail station without encountering anything out of the ordinary, but I wouldn't relax until I was safely hidden from the streets in my own room. The way things were going, I couldn't let my guard down.

The ride to the center of the city was quiet, and finding a hotel that overlooked the square where the drop was scheduled to take place wasn't too difficult at this time of year. As I stood on the balcony looking down on the square, I peered into the morning bustle of people heading to their day jobs, searching the faces for anything that stood out. An inquiry into the online activities of the buyer and my handler came up empty, which began to worry me. Not responding for a few hours after acquiring the target was one thing. No answer after almost a day was a bad sign.

From the balcony, I walked back into the large hotel room. The immense thick bed had been soft and comfortable, and the room service brought a breakfast fit for a king. A sheepish grin spread across my face as I thought this was how I should be living, not in some dumpy out-of-the-way hole in the wall apartment on the edge of town.

Regardless of the comfort of the bed, sleep had only come in fits as my mind fought to make sense of things. The drop was still a few hours away, but my instincts were already telling me to run and find a buyer that I knew wasn't tied up in the events of the past day. That was my clue to prepare the ground for what I imagined would be an inevitable betrayal. Too many unforeseen problems had arisen, and this op was beginning to spin beyond my control. My chance to change the course of events in my favor was now.

As in real estate, when you're planning to steal corporate secrets, it's all about location, location, location. I'd made sure the drop point was in a high traffic area with multiple exits and sightlines. The beautiful thing was that only two people besides myself – my handler and the client – knew the actual location.

I found a vantage point at a corner cafe that gave me a chance to watch the local business people come and go. Everyone looked the same: the latest fashion in suits and dresses, briefcases, purses and expensive shoes. They also behaved similarly, hurrying to wherever they were going with little concern for what was going on around them. The advantage in everyone looking the same was that it would be easier to pick out the ones that didn't belong.

I'd set the drop time to occur during lunchtime, because it was the busiest time of the day, and there would be lots of people on and along the streets to camouflage our activity. Being on my own and not able to call in support put me on edge while I watched.

When it was finally time to make the drop, I paid my bill and walked slowly into the flowing crowd. I was to wait on a very specific bench for the client. They would sit on the other end of the bench, seemingly uninterested in me. They were supposed to have my payment in a black briefcase that they would set on the ground between us. I would be pretending to eat my lunch, setting a bag with the merchandise on the bench between us. The client would nonchalantly take the bag, check the contents and leave me with the briefcase.

That was the plan, that had been the plan before two different times someone tried to capture or kill me. Keeping pace with a group of businessmen walking through the center of the park, I utilized them as camouflage, like a predator using a herd of elk to hide his approach to a better prey. Once close to the drop point, I took a seat at a nearby bench, which gave me a good line of sight. Pulling out a news datapad, I quietly pretended to read.

It didn't take long for me to realize how royally fragged I was. At the far end of the park a pair of large sleek black transports pulled up to the curb and stopped. Four men exited the vehicles; dark glasses, black suits and angry expressions told me everything I needed to know about their intentions. They moved closer up the walkway, with the two rear men splitting up onto the right and left walkways, keeping their sightlines with the front men clear. They were blocking the routes out, in order to trap their quarry.

Realizing that this was where all of my planning would work out, I stood, tucking the datapad into my jacket. I turned toward the two men on the walkway, moving with the flow of traffic. The men were searching the benches for familiar faces, or for someone eating a lunch. It was lucky for me that my paranoia and instinct overruled my need to end the op.

I kept my demeanor plain and calm, walking easily up the path towards the approaching men. Only a few feet from the men, I saw them scanning the faces without truly seeing anything. The largest of the four men, the person I deemed to be in charge, stood in the middle of the walk with his side to me as he signaled one of the men further out.

The flow of people up and down the walk didn't seem to change. The men stood out, but not enough to warrant looks from most of the people on the street. As I approached the assumed leader, preparing to pass him and make my escape, I had to shift my movement to the right to allow a woman nudging past the man to go by. That was when all hell broke loose.

As I moved aside, the woman's chest imploded in a bloom of red, spraying blood in every direction behind her. She flew back into the lead man, and his training kicked in. Instantly, he crouched, pulling his weapon from his jacket. Screams filled the air as people ran in every direction, diving behind trash cans, benches and bushes.

The shot that hit the woman had startled me, my instincts kicked in as I dove for a nearby trash can, watching as chaos took over the park. The sound of a ricochet off of the metal pulled me back into reality, and I realized that the first shot had been intended for me, not the man or woman. That was when it dawned on me that there were two players in this game, not just one.

The four men all started shouting over the screams of the crowd as they began running in the direction of the shots. I took this moment to make an exit, in the hope that my assailant was more concerned with being tracked than killing his target. Keeping myself low, I moved along a line of benches and bushes until I couldn't hide anymore.

There were ten meters between me and the edge of the closest wall. Ten meters I would have to run in hopes that whoever had been shooting was more concerned with the armed men in the street than with me. The throng of running and screaming pedestrians was beginning to subside, so I knew I needed to take a chance before I became a lone target on an open field.

The sound of gunfire erupted behind me, which I assumed came from the four security men. Taking my cue, I launched myself forward, running straight for the corner of the building. Gunfire continued as I ran, crouched as much as possible without ruining my momentum. The wall grew closer and closer and I just knew I was going to catch a bullet the instant before I reached it.

I ran like I was at the end of a marathon with the finish line in sight, and all I had to do was not collapse before I reached it. Ten meters seemed like a hundred, time seemed to slow as my lungs burned in my chest and blood pulsed in my ears. I burst past the corner of the building; a spray of brick greeted me as a piece of the building's corner exploded less than a foot from my head, but nothing in my body signaled I had been hit by anything other than flying brick shards.

No matter how much my chest hurt or my heart churned inside my chest, I kept moving until I knew I was safely removed from the firefight. Lights flashing and sirens blaring, security and emergency vehicles fought their way through retreating civilians, headed for the square. As soon as I had a chance, I waved down a ride, jumped in and pointed the driver toward the space port while I hunkered down in the seat to keep a low profile.

I hated to admit that I expected a need to escape the planet quickly and disappear. I hated that I had to plan ahead by leaving my bags at the Spaceport and buying a seat on an outbound transport. I was frustrated that things had gone downhill so fast that I couldn't keep ahead of the problems, but I realized I had to drop off the grid long enough to find a solution to my problems.

****

The busy street outside, filled with groups of young adults in skimpy dresses and fancy suits hurrying off to bars or parties, gave me a perfect cover. My natural camouflage, plus the opportunity to mix in with other people, gave me the chance to hide myself from any surveillance that might be looking for me, as well as get lost in my thoughts again.

The incongruities of the evening were starting to pile up, forming a mystery. My mind normally enjoyed mysteries, curiosity was one of the side-effects of my enhancements, but they were dangerous for a man in my line of work. No matter how I followed the line of events leading up to this moment, like a rat lost in a maze, I continued to run into walls.. Who were the soldiers working for? They weren't corp security. How had they known I was there? Had the explosion been a countermeasure, or had the soldiers triggered something? A pit began growing in my stomach as my instincts warned me that something was amiss.

A torrent of rain bathed the city as I walked, causing me to turn up the collar of my coat. I picked up my pace as people ran in every direction to escape the downpour. My senses were on high alert for anything out of the ordinary, but the rain made the otherwise deserted streets difficult to read. After a time, I reached familiar territory: the neighborhood near my safe house.

The rain had stopped as I grew closer, my natural tendency would have been to relax and feel safe, yet my instincts tended to be right about situations, and this time, the pit in my stomach grew stronger as I walked up the sidewalk along a large red brick warehouse across from my safe house. This neighborhood was not a place that a lone person should have been wandering at night. I normally wouldn't have stayed in a rough neighborhood like this one, made up of low-income apartments and abandoned industrial buildings, but my handler thought it would be a nice way to "lay low" during an op.

I slowed my pace as I approached the corner of the building. A broken street lamp and recessed doorway created an ideal vantage point from which I could scan the street. The deserted street was eerily quiet and devoid of all but the occasional foot traffic, and homeless residents.

I'd spent a week watching the people come and go to make sure I knew what this area's "normal" looked like. My initial sweep of the street began to set my mind at ease, if not the knot in my stomach. It wasn't until I was about to step out onto the lit street that I caught a glint of light from further down the street Partially hidden in the shadow of heavy ferro-steel girders that supported the cities light rail, a small dark vehicle caught my eye. .

Had it not been for a street lamp's unexpected flicker of life, I would never have noticed the vehicle, which was out of place in this part of town. I barely made out the form of a man sitting in the driver seat. He parked in a way to watch the street from a non-descript vantage point. At this point, my instincts screamed high alert. I scanned the street again. If I had missed the vehicle, I wondered what else I had missed. Nothing else stood out on the street, but that brought up another question: Why would they send a lone person after they had already sent an assault team? Were these two even related?

I fought with myself about what I should do. To leave and come back another time would be the safe move, but if I did that, I'd lose this chance to verify my paranoia, and I'd likely sacrifice my gear in the safe house. While I told myself that material things are replaceable, my curiosity wouldn't be stymied regarding the real threat.

Nature took over as I decided to risk it. I guessed the amount of time it would take for someone to reach the safe house door after I entered. I'd have just enough time. As nonchalant as possible, I stepped out scanning the street as if looking for traffic before I crossed toward the door to the safe house. I kept the vehicle in my peripheral view, to make sure the occupant hadn't started to pursue me.

At the door, I activated the key card locking mechanism, which welcomed me with a buzz and a click as the door opened. Inside, I turned to close the door and activate the double locking system, but that would hold someone for only a minute or two, not longer. I moved into the living room, grabbing the two large duffels on the center table. My pace quickening, I walked into the bedroom, then the closet. I pulled a square of carpet aside to reveal a large metal door in the floor.

Pulling the door open, I dropped the bags down and followed closely behind, replacing the door behind me. The carpet would fall back into place, just as I had designed it to do. One of the advantages of having the company backing my ops was that I tended to get low-key safe houses with features that make it a true "safe" house. I began moving along the tunnel lit by a small line of soft krylon lights.

My timing couldn't have been better. I made it into the tunnel just as three muffled pops reverberated through the floor. A crash resembling metal and wood torn from a wall, followed immediately by three more loud pops, made me jump. I moved quicker along the small square space, hoping to reach the exit before whoever was in the apartment found the hatch.

Finally, the destination appeared: a large metal door with no handles or knobs. Only a key card slot with a number pad below gave any indication that the door would open. Inserting my card and punching in my code, a muffled thud released the door, which slowly swung open into a sewer maintenance shaft a few hundred meters from the house in a direction that would be hard to discern from outside of the actual tunnel.

Pulling myself and the duffels into the shaft, the door closed behind me and the same muffled thud signaled the door had locked. I followed the maintenance shaft for about ten minutes before I found an exit point, which opened to a fairly run-down collection of warehouses and factories. I found myself a building with a heavy metal door that swung open just enough for me to enter. Satisfied that I was safe for the moment, I fought to bring my heart rate back down and concentrate on what I needed to do

I rested for a moment, letting my heart rate settle and my mind focus on the problem, and my next priority: finding a safe place to lay low until I could drop off the Cypher and figure out what was going on. I ran the layout of the city through my mind via one of the other advantages of my transformation: eidetic memory. Knowing I was in the southwest industrial region, I figured out the fastest way to the part of town closest to the drop point, then figured out which hotels were in that area and how to get to them.

****

Getting off planet hadn't been difficult; the transport took off without delay, one of my many aliases clearing me through security with a valid reason for having secret tech tucked away in my luggage. The trick was where to go next. If my support network and mission coordination had truly been compromised, I couldn't rely on my usual channels to find answers.

I held Cypher up in front of my eyes, letting the overhead light of the soft first class seat fracture through the crystal. This one little piece of engineered glass had turned into the bane of my existence, and nothing I did brought me any closer to getting rid of it. How had the soldiers known I'd be in the office? Who was shooting at whom at the drop? Questions ran randomly through my mind, trying to figure out what to do and how all of the pieces fit together. The only common element was the Cypher, but I still didn't know how it mattered or how they might be tracking it.

I turned away from the crystal to stare out the viewport as the planet slowly grew smaller and the transport slipped smoothly into the local trade lane, thrown forward at such speeds that the stars blurred into streaks against the blackness of space. It was going to take the better part of two days to reach the transfer station. From there, I could go anywhere: farther out toward the rim world, farther in toward the Republic's core worlds, or even disappear into Androken space.

Unfortunately, as much as I wanted to vanish into the ether and hope my assailants might forget about me, there was something inside me that ate at me, feeding a need to solve this riddle. We'd all but arrived at the transfer point when I finally decided where I needed to go.

There were only a handful of people I knew who were far enough outside my normal support network that I could be reasonably sure they weren't compromised. As I considered the short list, I concluded that there was only one person I knew who had the expertise to find the information I needed, and who could also find me a way to get rid of this ball-and-chain merchandise. When I reached the station, I booked a transport to the Republic's outer core planet, Sanctuary. The trip would take a few days, but my hope was that that would be enough time for my contact on the planet to set up a meet.

I found an open interweb terminal and sat down. Knowing that my usual system access could be tracked, I inserted a second crystal I had picked up from an asset a few years back. It gave me the same level of access, but could not be tracked by the company. As soon as I logged in, I reached out, looking for clues or information to point me in a direction.

At the same time, I logged into a site I knew my contact used regularly and sent him a message;

Cyberjunky –

Lost your number, would really like to talk. Traveling for a few days but free for kava when I get back. The three moons here are blood red and it's Really Ass Hot. Hope to see you soon.

– Harlequin.

I smiled briefly as I looked over the message. There wasn't anything in the message that would stand out, but there was enough to point him in the right direction.

Kava at the Three Moons Café in Sanctuary's capital city had been our meet point the last time I had used him on a mission. One of the downsides of being an operative was the need to keep track of all the aliases I had had, as well as all the assets I had ever had contact with, in case I needed to work with them again. On the bright side, Kelvis Trena had never been an asset as much as he had been last-minute support for a job, which meant he didn't cross the company's radar.

Four days, three way stations, and two false alarms that I was being followed finally turned into a boarding call for a flight leaving Freeport Five for Sanctuary. Freeport Five was a deep-range space station between Republic Space and the Republic's colony system called the Drandelion Freehold.

Freeport Five was one of seven waystations between the Trokus core, home of the Trokus Republic, and its outlying colonies. Each station provided a location for the regions merchants to trade goods and services to travelers moving back and forth. Each station also maintained a hyperspace jumpgate that allowed near-instantaneous travel between the edges of the two systems. Republic trade lanes made up a large "rail" system, providing hyperlight acceleration for smaller ships that weren't able to generate the massive power required for hyperlight travel inside the systems. While traveling from one side of a system to another would usually take years, hyperlight acceleration turned that into hours or days depending on the size of the system. All ships relied on the massive jumpgate network to travel between systems.

As the transport turned from the station toward the jumpgate, its massive dimensions came into view. Monstrous gold wings, which collected untold amounts of energy to generate the vortex ships used to jump, shimmered in the system's red dwarf sun. The wondrous generators formed an almost perfect oval around the void where the shimmering energy swirled.

As our ship turned, another moved into position to jump. The almost insubstantial field forming the blue lightning that jumped from one generator to the next fluctuated like the heat of a desert valley. The stars behind moved with the shifting light as the ship drifted into the field and disappeared with a flash. A moment later, the field wavered again as a small transport appeared on the event horizon of the vortex. As the transport turned between the pylons, our turn came. The ship drew closer and closer to the generators as the blue lightning increased in power, until we finally drifting into the field.

The millisecond that it actually took for the ship to travel from one system to the other seemed like a long moment of extended black and calm as the blackness of space behind the jumpgate became the planet of Sanctuary. The massive asteroid field that drifted close to Sanctuary's orbit drove the many reasons for the jumpgate's proximity to the planet. In most systems, jumpgates were located at the edges, with trade lanes carrying ships to the major stations or planets.

The large foreboding greenish-blue planet loomed in space. From space, I could see the numerous craters, the results of many random asteroid impacts, line the northern hemisphere. Sanctuary's major landmass covered almost seventy-five percent of the planet's surface; leaving little moisture in the atmosphere. Oddly enough, an abundant supply of water existed below the surface in the form of underground lakes.

Sanctuary had once been the last refuge of political dissidents and revolutionaries escaping a war on the Trokus system's main planet of Anderia, in the days before the Republic stretched into the stars. I marveled at the view as it hung in space, its four moons circling in slow methodical orbits. Two of the moons had been part of the nearby asteroid belt. Eventually caught in Sanctuary's gravitational pull, they settled into high orbits around the planet.

As we turned in toward the planet and picked up speed, my mind drifted back to the problem at hand. Kelvis had confirmed the meeting; I just hoped that he could help to illuminate the situation.

Landing in Sanctuary City's main starport with little fanfare, the main core of the city to the north was lit up with multiple displays in various colors and styles. Holographic billboards flashed advertisements from the latest in home appliances and cerebral implants to casino games and hair care products. All the while, transports and personal vehicles created a thousand multi-colored stars in the air above the city.

Exiting the spaceport, the parched air burned in my lungs. It reminded me how much I had despised the planet's seasons the last time I had been here. I hailed a cab to the center of town and settled into the seat. My mind raced with information I had, as well as the holes that needed filler.

Once in the Relagen district, the ritzy-glitzy part of town, old patterns began to take over as I headed toward a hotel I had used on two earlier trips to Sanctuary. Reluctant to pick habit over security, I picked a less chic hotel further down the street. This wasn't something I liked to do, but then the circumstances called for doing thing out of the ordinary.

The room was smaller than I was used to, but I'd make due considering the circumstance. I spent a few minutes getting the feel for the room and checking for surveillance devices. It could be considered paranoid when I thought about it, but after the week I'd had, I couldn't take chances. A quick shower and a change of clothes later, I stepped out onto the bustling city street, breathing in the warm evening summer air.

All manner of wheeled and hover vehicles zoomed past, their drivers oblivious to the city around them. I walked along the street as crowds of people weaved in and out of each other, bound for destinations unknown. People dressed in business suits heading home from work, as well as people dressed in slick, fashionable clothes on their way to a party or club, crowded the streets as I walked.

My attire was stylish but plain in comparison to those around me, which was intentional. How I dressed was a way to hide in plain sight. Flashy attire drew attention, and now was not the time for attention. I strolled through city streets, taking in the ambiance and keeping my eyes and ears open for anything out of the ordinary. Upon reaching the part of town I was looking for, I smiled when I saw the small café set into the corner of an apartment building located where the high-end residential and commercial areas came together.

The Three Moons was a local favorite, with a regular crowd of patrons. Kelvis and I had used it the last time I was on Sanctuary to pass mission details. The warm homey café feeling made it easy for two people to talk in private and not raise suspicions. Wondering if Kelvis had arrived first, I entered. The heavy aroma of kava and steamed borva filled my nostrils, bringing a smile to my face as I moved through the lounge area.

I ordered a small kava drink and settled into one of the soft plush chairs along the side wall of the lounge where I could see the doors. As I sat and inhaled the aroma, I stared down at the cup in my hand. The off-white borva foam mixed with the soft brown kava to form a gentle, mesmerizing pattern. It occurred to me that I hadn't had fresh Kava in a few weeks.

I sipped my drink as my eyes scrutinized the random patrons and my ears gathered whatever tidbits of information I felt could be useful for later. It didn't take long for Kelvis to arrive. He grinned as he entered, I presumed from catching me sitting inside already, but showing little acknowledgment of my presence. His tall broad frame had the look of an athlete. Kelvis kept his long brown hair pulled back in a ponytail, causing the angular lines of his cheeks and jaw to stand out all the more. A pair of wire-rimmed glasses sat on his hawkish nose, and the soft blue tint of the lenses kept his eyes hidden. He wore baggy pants and a pull-over top with a hood, which allowed him to blend in well with the laid-back patrons.

After ordering his drink, Kelvis moved to the back of the cafe. I took that as my cue to join him. The seating arrangement caused me to smirk. He had picked a seat that was far away from any doors or windows, yet provided him a good sightline to both. We sat with our backs to the wall, yet kept space between us in case of a hasty exit. It would have been obvious to another operative what we were. Kelvis nodded as I sat, his expression held the small smile from when he entered, as if my appearance had been part of a joke he heard earlier in the day.

"I'm glad to see you got my message." My voice resonated low enough to mix in with the natural chatter in the cafe. "I'd hate to think I came all the way out here for nothing except a chance to drop off the grid."

My comment caused a slight shift in the muscles in his face, something a normal person may not have noticed, but something hard to hide from me. "If you're running from someone, I'm not sure I can help. Your targets tend to be a little out of my league."

I frowned. He knew that I knew his true purpose on Sanctuary, and where he got his support. "To be honest, I just need two things. I need a quiet way to contact my handler, and I need a buyer for a hot piece of tech I'd like to get rid of without a hassle. I'm sure a few corps in the Freehold would be eager to buy it."

Behind his glasses, I could see the edges of his eyes wrinkle as he considered the situation. Kelvis was a fixer, a black market jack-of-all-trades who found solutions to his clients' problems; his general modus operandi would be to put them in touch with operators like me. What most of his clients didn't know was that he was also a mole for the Republic, always trying to get a sense of the black market players who used the Freehold and Sanctuary as their playground.

Kelvis had connections that most people in his place wouldn't have, and I knew it.

"What can you tell me about the tech?" he whispered from behind the cup he held up to his mouth.

"Biogen recently lost a DNA lockable organic data crystal. The news doubtless reported it as a malfunction during a test that destroyed the western wing of one of their research labs on Talmeria. But I assure you, I have it."

Kelvis nodded a little as I talked, taking mental notes of the situation and likely already thinking about how he could go about filling the request. "I take it you've tried to contact your handler through the usual channels?"

I nodded.

"And I assume back channels aren't working because you're concerned about how compromised you are?"

I nodded again, knowing that Kelvis' handle on how things are should be good enough.

"Are you staying nearby? Where can I get a hold of you when I figure out what I can offer you?"

Realizing the meeting was ending, I sipped the last of my Kava. "I'm at the Polaris Hotel, under Robert Hamilton. When you have something, leave me a message and we'll meet back here."

Kelvis nodded in agreement. "Sounds good," he said with a smile. "It'll probably be a day or two before I have anything. Try to keep your head down."

He upturned his glass, draining the creamy brown liquid. Without further conversation, he walked toward the door. I watched as he left, making sure no one was paying too much attention to his departure, then I stood and made my way toward the door.

****

I had spent much of the next two days wandering the streets and searching through the web traffic for my usual contacts. It was intimidating that the deeper I looked, the more I realized everything was out of sorts. As I tried to put all the pieces together, nothing seemed to fit well enough to form a picture. There wasn't all of the usual web traffic from other operatives and handlers. After years of regular use, I had grown familiar with difference between seemingly random user and covert activity, and there hadn't been any covert traffic to speak of for the last week.

I couldn't think of a reason why all operative traffic would stop without notice, which bothered me even more. I needed answers and all I seemed to find were more questions. I hadn't heard from my handler in over a week. Had we been burned, or just compromised? The gravity of the situation was weighing on me. After almost ten years of service, I was suddenly without support on a planet I'd worked on only twice. I was a little bit anxious about the whole situation, regardless of what my calm demeanor showed.

On the bright side, I had a habit of siphoning large portions of my operational credits to ghost accounts throughout Republic space, to ensure that I would never be short on funds or resources in a bad situation. Thanks to a cyber-accountant, I had started using several years ago on an operation, moving credits without footprints had become quite an easy job. The real question was how long being on the run would become a way of life for me.

Being cut off and alone was having an effect on my psyche, which illuminated the elation I felt when I received Kelvis' note to meet. It was ironic that the location he chose was a local museum dedicated to the drive and determination of the colonists who escaped persecution and war on the home planet of Anderia and moved to Sanctuary to be free of the sentiment of the Republic's greedy expansionist drive.

I was studying the Sanctuary Charter, which established the lead government of Sanctuary and their stance on Republic interference, when Kelvis stepped up beside me.

"They really had rather vocal feelings about the Republic back then, didn't they?" he whispered, not showing any sign of acknowledging my presence.

Before I could reply, he turned and moved deeper into the more isolated exhibits of the museum. I turned to follow him, but stayed back, stopping at intermittent artifacts and pieces of art before moving toward him. We entered a deeper section of the museum that housed the exhibit on the history of Sanctuary before, during and after its terraforming and eventual colonization. Some displays discussed the environment of the planet and how it affected the process of terraforming, along with what the process, while others talked of the struggles of the first colonists to find the resources to live.

While I found much of this interesting, the lack of patrons in this part of the museum led me to believe that it wasn't the most popular exhibit. Kelvis stood near the far wall, looking at a large laser-etched crystal display of the planet and its moons. By my understanding, the moons were important due to their very abnormal effect on the planet's atmosphere and gravity. The display faced the far wall, which kept our conversation hidden from onlookers.

"You have no idea how hard it was to get this information for you. Many of the normal channels are being monitored or locked."

"I know. I made several inquiries of my own since we last met, and it wasn't encouraging."

Kelvis smiled at my comment as if he knew something I didn't. "I have a buyer for your item. He's on Taldera. I've worked with him before, so I'm not sending you to a random buyer whom I've never met. He'll give you a good deal. I've set the meeting for four days from today. That'll give you enough time to get into Drandelion space and set things in motion. As for the other part, I have what I could find."

He held out a small data crystal. "It's not a lot, but it should get you close enough to figure out parts to the puzzle. The buyer's info is on the crystal, too."

I looked down at the small smooth crystal rod. It wasn't an explanation wrapped up with a bow and ribbon, but to expect that would have been out of character for me. I palmed the crystal, holding it between my fingers until I had a chance to slip it somewhere secure.

"Thank you, Kelvis. You've never left me hanging in the past. It's good to know I have at least one person I can turn to in a bind." I smiled, thinking that at least I was no longer alone in trying to solve this puzzle.

"I'll keep looking. If I find anything, I'll contact you through the channels you used. I'll figure out a way to embed it or transmit it to you."

"It's always a pleasure working with you my friend," I responded, reaching over to offer my hand. "Stay safe."

He returned the handshake. "You too, Rah. Good luck." He turned away from our meeting place, his nonchalant path carrying him through the exhibit.

I stood quietly staring at the display, turning the crystal between my fingers as I thought considered my next steps.

My thoughts wandered as I walked the city, stopping eventually at a local interweb café. I committed the information for the buyer from Kelvis' crystal to memory, then I opened the details Kelvis had given me about my handler. He was right, it wasn't much, but it pointed me in a direction, which was more than I had. There were keywords and clues that pointed me to a planet, and other information that pointed me to where I might find him. Since contacting him wasn't working, a face-to-face conversation would be necessary.

I wiped the crystal and cleared any record of my access. It was never a good idea to leave any trace of a search, and the fact that I needed to do all of this on a public terminal meant that further compromise was likely.

I headed back toward the hotel to grab my things and book a ride off-planet. A trip to Taldera would be three days, assuming no issues. "No issues" generally relied on the Drandelion trader guilds keeping the space lanes into the Freehold from Sanctuary clear of pirates or scavengers. On the bright side, if this contact gave me my asking price for the Cypher, I'd be more than set to track down the answers I needed.

The midday streets were bustling with business as I flagged down a taxi. "To the spaceport, and there's an extra fifty credits in it for you if you get me there fast."

The driver wasted no time revving his engine and squealing down the street. A high speed vehicle moving through traffic would be harder to follow but more easily seen.

My hand turned Kelvis' crystal over and over inside my pocket as my mind ran through the nuggets of information he had given me. I knew the crystal was blank. The only copy of the information was now in my mind. The sense of the direction that his information had given me became the first comfort I'd felt in weeks.

ACT TWO

Mr. Hood stood stoically behind the case that carried his terminal. He'd pushed several buttons and keys on whatever interface he had connected to the system before placing the Cypher in the test machine. As he placed the crystal in the slot, a dark shadow drifted over his eyes. His brow furrowed more and more with each passing second as his eyes looked at me, then back to the display. The eventual look of intense anger filled his face along with what I was guessing was blood under his skin as his hand reached inside his jacket.

What happened next broke into a slow motion moment seen in vids, which was why it turned out to be such a tragic yet comical event. I noticed his hand as it tightly gripped and pulled the butt end of a pistol out of his jacket. His eyes locked on me, the flush red skin grew darker. Just as the gun broke the fold of his coat, the world exploded into a flurry of action and debris. The display on his case shattered outward toward him as something punched through the back of the case.

Glass and ferroplastic and metal exploded into the surrounding air. At the same time, several other items shattered into pieces as I noticed the unmistakable report of weapon rounds impacting nearby. The next moment, his chest blossomed into a splash of dark red as a large gouge appeared just below his collarbone.

My instincts took over, and I immediately took cover. Thankful he'd set his case down by a thick ferroscrete block wall, I hunkered low, trying to regain my composure.

As Mr. Hood fell to the ground, his case followed him. As time sped up to normal, clutter, shrapnel and debris rained around me. I looked down to see the Cypher and the credit chip he brought to the exchange lying on the ground in the shattered case. The report of rounds still tearing into ferroscrete filled the air, three-round bursts by my last count.

I snatched up the Cypher and the credit chip, stuffed them into my coat pocket, and pulled the pistol from Mr. Hood's hand. My assailants would be on me in seconds. I had to find a clear path out or I was following the late Mr. Hood. After my eyes adjusted to the dull moonlight, I searched the few other walls nearby that I could use for cover. A run along them might expose me for a few moments, but it was better than the alternative.

My heart thumped in my chest and blood rapped at my ears as I waited for a lull in the shooting. I hoped they were reloading or looking for new targets. I took a deep breath, knowing that I couldn't hit a thing with my heart racing.

Four random shots from Mr. Hood's gun in the general direction of the assailants signaled my departure. I took off running, my hand behind me squeezing off more shots. To my amazement, the return fire impacted the wall I ran past, close enough to my head to feel the impacts.

It was fortunate that we planned the exchange at night in a secluded location. A lack of the normal daytime security presence at this moment was a good thing. There wouldn't be a problem with scared civilians clamoring for cover. The downside was that I was running blind in the dark toward an uncertain escape route. I only hoped that my assailants were just as blind.

Four or five more reports echoed behind me, but I ran ducking low. Fearful trepidation propelled me forward expecting the burning pain of a bullet to pierce my skin at any instant. When no burning or pain came, I counted my lucky stars and kept moving, hoping that my preparation before the meeting was enough to get me out. These circumstances were a stark reminder of the disadvantage of my job: a lack of any large well-stocked support network to help me.

Several vehicles traveled through the nearby woods. The sound of nearby shouting caused me to shift my escape to a more perpendicular route from my previous direction and the meeting site. I hoped the change in direction would throw off my pursuers enough to find a nice discreet hiding place in the darker areas.

It disheartened me that I had reached this point: alone in the dark, running for my life, and now squeezed into a storm drain half my size. I sat quietly in the cold muddy water trying not to get killed, thinking about the events that had led me to this point.

I waited silently, listening to the sounds of men yelling and the echoes of their radios filtering through the still night air. The voices grew closer, then farther away. It was hard to know how many men I was evading, but I knew the odds were not in my favor.

A twig snapped near me, then a green laser light, just perceptible in the moonlight, swept back and forth through the trees. I could hear movement through the underbrush a few meters away. The source of the laser light came into view as I watched from my hole. Clad in black, the soldier stepped into the clearing. He was almost invisible, except for the small breaks of moonlight through the trees.

Focused on my breathing, I kept my calm while concentrating on altering his perception. With my talent, I could create passionate attraction in someone or make them turn on their best friend as easily as smiling at them. The simple effects that were a part of the body's natural reaction were always much easier and less taxing to manipulate. Affecting someone's mind to see or not see something right in front of their eyes, well, that was a trick that took time to master. The best I could figure out was that the effect played with the perceptive regions of the mind, creating or blocking visual cues. It was a trick I had learned about a year before. I couldn't have imagined the genetic modifications they made would be so vital in such a life-threatening circumstance.

He approached the storm drain, stopping less than two meters from the opening. If he looked close, a shift of light between the metal of the drain and my body may have exposed me. He took two more steps, his rifle pointed at the ground, the green laser a less than a meter from me.

The soldier stood frozen. The tension in my body grew as I considered that I may not have affected him. I knew the range of my talent was limited in outdoor environments. The tension pulled at me more and more while he stood over me. Just as my hand raised the gun to the man point blank in front of me, mind working alternative escape plans, the soldier turned away, moving back out of the clearing and into the trees.

The burning in my chest grew uncomfortable, reminding me that I had been holding my breath. Slowly and steadily, I exhaled. My heart raced in my chest as the sound of my pulse pounded in my ears. I slipped out of the drain, hoping the soldiers had moved away. My heart began the slow steady descent back to acceptable levels, as adrenaline fed the tension in my muscles with energy. I kept myself low in the shadows, paying close attention to the noises around me as I moved.

I crept for what seemed like all night, cursing myself for thinking the park being less extensive than this. My original preparation for the meeting hadn't taken into account vehicles and armed soldiers. Then again, the realities of plans never seem to work out the way you imagine them.

Exhilaration filled me as I reached a clearing, giving me hope that I might be out of the woods, literally and figuratively. The two shiny black transports sitting at an intersection along the edge of the park dashed much of that hope.

The difficult part of convincing someone I wasn't there was often the ability to hide from their sight. Watching me run across a lit road in the middle of the night wasn't going to keep them from seeing me, no matter how much I wanted them not to.

Another unfortunate element of the ability was the toll it took on my body. With normal physical activity, my blood was somewhat normal and didn't require attention, aside from a daily dose of Promium to keep me clean. Using my ability in small chunks still required a daily dose of Promium, but it wore me out physically. To push my ability to the level needed to convince someone I'm not standing near them generally required an immediate dose of Promium. It also required at least eight hours of sleep before I could get back to my normal cheery self.

Considering what I had to do to escape, lurking in the woods in the middle of the night would not end well for someone with my condition. Hidden by shadows, I leaned against a tree and considered my options. Unfortunately, there weren't many. I could follow the edge of the trees until I was far enough out of sight to escape. Of course, that assumed there wasn't another group on the road.

To my utter dismay, my need for options evaporated as four black-clad soldiers exited the tree line not far from where I sat, then climbed into vehicles. Within a few minutes, they drove away. Being as paranoid as I was after all of this, I waited until I was sure they were truly gone and not a trick to lure me out of the woods..

The numbness in my mind, the burning blood in my veins, and the exhaustion in my body forced me to move. I stepped from the tree line and worked my way to the nearest public street. Thankfully, I didn't have to wait long for a ride.

"The Hendron House, please," I said as I laid back in the soft padded seat.

As the vehicle moved, I pulled a small auto-injector from my coat pocket. Applying medicine to the exposed skin in my neck, I sighed, feeling the liquid warm my blood. My eyes closed and my thoughts drifted back to the moments before the buyer's chest exploded all over the merchandise.

Why had he looked unhappy? What would have caused him to pull a gun on me? Had Kelvis set me up? As that last question hung in my mind, another realization crossed my mind: I never had a chance to have the crystal tested to verify that it was the genuine article.

It never crossed my mind how quickly the soldiers had arrived in the office. As I thought about it, it seemed odd how long the airborne transport had been on approach even before they arrived. It didn't take me long to realize that the crystal was the problem, not the soldiers or the bad intelligence.

I didn't like the direction that my thoughts were going, but I'd always understood the problem with this business. The absence of logical answers to a problem tended to lend itself to the more illogical possibilities.

Had the Cypher been the bait? Had it been the trap that exposed our network? Was my capture supposed to clear the books? The plasma blast had seemed a bit extreme as a countermeasure at the time. Had I been captured by the soldiers, I would have been in the room with them when the blast went off, clean and simple. My mind started racing as the pieces of the puzzle fell into place.

Had the man outside the safehouse been a failsafe in the event that I escaped? The next piece of the puzzle that I couldn't explain was how they found both of the drop sites. The first was easy in that they had compromised our network, so once they understood our codes, they knew the drop. The second was more of a mystery, but I started to build a picture.

Merchandise of this nature would need verification. A man with the resources to buy merchandise like this would certainly use those resources to check the validity of the claim before agreeing to a buy. It was highly likely that the channels he used to verify the merchandise also reached back to whoever was directing the troops. These men were not likely Corp security, so the only option was private contractors. The thought didn't sit well in my mind as the car came to a slow stop in front of the hotel.

I decided not to waste any time. I found a banking terminal nearby. I wanted to ensure that my loss didn't turn into a wasted effort. I may not be able to get rid of the Cypher, but I wasn't going to give up the chance to get paid for my efforts. I slid my utilities crystal into the port and the program in the crystal took over, giving me access to backdoor systems that I could use to access the new credit chip. I popped the late Mr. Hood's chip into the port, and the software I implemented slowly worked the encryption on the crystal until it finally broke through.

All of this would have been simpler if I'd bothered to bring my skimmer, I could have simply scanned the credit chip and transferred the funds, but not being sure how the transaction would be made, I deemed it unnecessary at the time. I smiled as the program highlighted the number of credits loaded on the account. I discerned that the Cypher was valuable, but I hadn't expected anything that extensive.

I activated the software, and the credit count on the crystal began to count down as the program made hundreds of thousands of small transfers across the interweb. Credits spread to phantom accounts that would divide out the balances across my hidden accounts. There wasn't any doubt in my mind that the credits were marked, but spreading them out and moving them around would eventually wipe the marks and block any attempts to track them.

As the account ticked down to zero I waited for a few minutes as the software worked its magic, and finally confirmed the dispersal of credits. I wasn't usually one to steal someone's assets unless it was a mission. I liked to think I still kept some scruples. I also liked to think that what I'd done up to that point was for the right reasons. Not that it mattered much. The late Mr. Hood wouldn't need the money anymore, and if I was truly compromised, I'd need every single credit to survive, to find out what happened.

I cleared the software from the banking system and took a leisurely walk back to my hotel, keeping a wary eye on my surroundings. This had been an agonizing few weeks with surprises and unanticipated visitors, so the last thing I needed was another bombshell. On top of that, my meeting with Mr. Hood had been hideously unproductive, so I wasn't looking forward to the final piece of my quest.

What were the chances they were watching my handler's suspected location? It stood to figure that this would turn out to be a trap and a dead end … in every sense!

I ambled through the streets, cultivating the seeds of material I had at my disposal; the location, the system, the details of how I'd been set up from the word "go." I knew there was every reason to believe that they would be waiting for me, but I also pondered the possibility that they were counting on me to never discover my handler's identity.

Why couldn't I just let this go, disappear into the rim worlds, use my skills for good or evil and simply cease to matter to whoever was involved? The possibility turned over and over in my mind. The one character trait that made me good for this line of work had also turned to be a decided weakness: my curiosity for unsolved mysteries and my need to solve them. This trait had served me well in the past, but this time, I feared it was going to get me killed.

The trip from the Freehold to Drellic would take two days, while a less obvious route would take five and have only limited exposure to local stations. The direct route would be more dangerous and go against my usual conservative nature, which seemed to be the one advantage I had against an enemy who knew my moves well, but I booked it anyway, using an identity I had made up a few years earlier during a side op that had no official sanction. Doing freelance work had seemed rather silly, seeing as we were freelance operatives to begin with, but the objective had been a noble cause I felt needed a champion. Ironically, this identity was now the champion I needed to survive this ordeal and find answers.

****

Much to my astonishment, I slept through a good deal of the trip. It never dawned on me how absolutely wrecked my body had become during the events of the past month.

No matter where on the transport I sat, the one nice thing about a window seat was the chance to see the planet come into view. There had always been something fresh and childishly curious about the expression on my face and the feeling in my heart whenever I entered a new system and saw the planets for the first time. This wasn't the first time I'd been to the Shenshi system, but it was the first time I'd been to Drellic, the fifth planet in a system of twelve, circling a rare dual suns that weren't binaries.

Shenshi had been the first system colonized by the Trokan Republic, and its magnitude was tremendous. With two non-binary suns and twelve planets of varying sizes and compositions, Shenshi represented a new prosperous start to many Trokan colonists who sought to explore the universe. Although only seven of the planets could sustain some level of life, the numerous mining and space stations over the uninhabitable worlds provided a great deal of variety to the bold explorer. Shenshi's key attraction was being on the border with the

Androckan Federation, which over the years had provided a steady flow of integration between the feline Androckans and the Trokan Republic population.

The large greyish blue planet hung bright against the deep black curtain of space. A number of dark metal stations and an assortment of large ships hanging from them slowly circled the large gray-blue planet. One massive vessel, larger than three or four stations combined, hung over the cool bluish white of Drellic's northern pole. The flat rectangular ship bristled with cannons and antennas along its seemingly endless spine, while smaller ships hung in its proximity. A Republic Navy dreadnought was there to let any would-be raiders know that Drellic was the headquarters of the Navy's expeditionary fleet.

Immense clusters of billowy white clouds draped over the planet's visible oceans and landmasses. Grey rocky continents sprinkled with distant patches of green lush land made up about half of the planet's landmass, while the rest seemed more hospitable and green. Expansive cities, visible even from orbit, dotted the continents' shorelines.

The cruiser slowed as it approached the planet, then turned softly toward a station with multiple flat round sections connected by small necks in between. Docking in space allowed the planetary governments to better control access and to save the transport companies money in fuel. Much to my surprise, docking and moving through customs happened rather quickly. It wasn't long before I was on a space elevator headed to the surface. I'd heard of these contraptions, but had never experienced one until now. To the best of my knowledge, some portion of the station is tethered to the planet, while a series of long powerful cables move people and equipment up and down to low planetary atmosphere in large shielded boxes.

The information Kelvis had given me told me that my handler was in the capital city of Drellic. The rest of the data had been fragmented and cryptic, but not useless. There were keywords and codewords that my handler had used to provide what I could only conclude was a status report. His last message read like an update on our latest mission. The key was the part where he had coded his current operations point, used for logistics and support, as well as my target location.

As I sat quietly in the back of the hired car, watching the ferrosteel structures and large modern buildings with glistening windows pass by,

I wondered if his last report had actually exposed us to the assassin. It had always stood to reason that someone had compromised our communications nodes, and thus our operation. However, this level of mission detail could have been an inside job. The prospect disturbed me more than I was willing to accept. Also, if the silence across our usual support structure was any indication, the whole system was gone.

"Stop here, please."

The driver pulled to the shoulder just a few blocks away from the location Kelvis gave me. It was apparent things hadn't been working in my favor as of late, and the last thing I wanted was to expose myself to more trouble. Paying the driver, I casually walked along the sidewalk while I carefully searched for anything out of the ordinary.

I neared the building I was looking for, which was across the street to my left. Certain that nothing unusual stood out, I darted across the street through traffic, then bounded up the building's stairs two at a time. The hairs on the back of my head stood up immediately as I tried the door and it opened. I wasn't sure if it was some feeling of impending danger, or the feeling of death coming from the apartment that made my hair stand on end; but I was sure the overpowering stench of death drove it home. Pulling my handkerchief over my face, I pushed into the dark musty apartment. It was drab, spartan décor. I found it curious that no one had been through to clean up the apartment, especially with the stench of decaying flesh filling the small space.

It didn't take long for me to find the source of the rank stench. The darkened back bedroom seemed more like a cave than a room. The air was thick; the room frozen in what I suspected was the same state the occupant had left it before his untimely demise. By the look of things, the assassin had struck in the middle of preparation for the op.

My handler's body sat slumped over a desk, face down on the keyboard with a black ferrocomposite dagger embedded in his back. Judging by the positioning of the dagger, the strike didn't kill him. As I looked over the scene, the large red stain under the chair and the deep red slice along his neck spoke to the true manner of death. The dagger in the back was a sign, not a killing blow.

Aside from the missing drive crystal and the destroyed computer terminal, the contents of the room were undisturbed. Doubting an interruption would arrive anytime soon, I began rummaging through the room, looking for anything that might point me in a useful direction.

Standing in the middle of the room, I noticed I was starting to grow accustomed to the stench of death, which was not a good thing. Having searched all of the obvious locations in the room for hidden information, my secretive mind sought places that most would not think to look. The problem I realized being how unlikely it was that my handler had any idea he had been compromised prior to the assassin's attack.

After a long moment of standing in the middle of the room staring at the contents, my eyes finally rested on the dagger embedded in my handler's back. Was he the key? Chances were he was a professional assassin, a professional who had a reputation. A reputation like that and a calling card like this could turn into a dangerous road.

I considered my options. I was off the grid now, I had enough resources to drop off further and go freelance without directions from on high. Why did it matter so much to me that the world I knew had been crushed and torn to shreds? Maybe it was the fact that I'd always be looking over my shoulder, always worried I was being hunted. Making them think I was dead or too much trouble to chase anymore would have been the smart play.

I grabbed the dagger and what little of the random items in the apartment that I thought might be useful before moving to the small kitchenette. Digging through the sparsely stocked cabinets, I found whatever I could that I thought would catch fire and threw it on top of the two thermal elements embedded into the countertop for cooking. Turning both on full power, I let them light the scrap and chemicals as I slipped out the back through the door to a long path running between rows of apartments. I walked nonchalantly away from the building as smoke began rising, blowing out glass and metal as fire overwhelmed the small building. Whatever they would find in the aftermath didn't matter to me anymore. The fire would warn my assassin that there were still people snooping.

****

I'd been sitting at a local interweb café, staring blankly at the little dot on the screen that beckoned me to insert words. I knew that whoever was chasing me had been given enough to fully compromise our operation. Clearly, there were a number of entities at work here, between the assassin and the men with guns. It was obvious they weren't working together, but their true intentions were murky at best, and the last thing I needed was for them to start working together.

The Cypher had to be the key to the soldiers. They had been the only group to show up at the drop with Mr. Hood. That could only mean they were tracking the Cypher, not me. Not completely unappealing, this prospect was one that could possibly represent an ace that I could play.

It crossed my mind that I'd lost the assassin when I went to Sanctuary because I was working a contact outside my normal patterns. In order to reach the assassin, I would have to go through the threads that my handler and I used to communicate. I wondered if he knew what I had found. Unless he was blind to my movements that didn't involve communication through regular channels, he probably did. Suffice it to say that my lack of confirmation on anything made this the only course of action.

The events of the past month circled in my mind as I considered my next steps. Almost as if by divine intervention, I remembered the missing crystal drive from the computer. Of all the things the assassin could have taken, it was the one thing that would allow him to track communications and net traffic. Putting my fingers on the keyboard, I constructed my message to my would-be killer.

Black Queen,

Missed our last move. The White Knight had pawns covering the board. I was able to avoid the Bishop, but had to sacrifice a Rook to escape. Need to retreat back to the Castle. The following moves should bring me home: Kxc4Ne3+46. Kc5Nxf547.

Bc7Ke648. Kb6Nd6.

Black Knight.

The board moves meant nothing to the casual observer and anyone who truly knew chess might try and figure out how the moves really worked. The key was in the crystals that the assassin took. If he knew enough about the operation, he'd know how to crack the coordinates. I hadn't left any time or date, which was intentional. If the assassin knew enough about the operation to compromise it, he'd know how the support and supply system had been set up. A series of drops and safe points set up on specific planets or stations. When support or resources were requested, the handler would arrange a drop and the operator would pick up when able.

If the assassin truly had lost track of me, he'd have no idea where I was or how long it would take me to arrive. The drop was on Haelstrom, a trade station in the Drandelion Freehold with controlled access I'd used many times in the past to vanish from pursuit. I'd picked Haelstrom because any transport from Drellic could reach the jump gate in a day. And unless the assassin was also on Drellic, it would be at least three days before he could reach the station.

That would give me time to prepare.

ACT THREE

Haelstrom was still the bustling port I remembered. It was the primary trade port between three Drandelion Freehold systems and Republic space, so there was always a heavy amount of traffic. The constant flow of people in and out played to one of my bigger advantages: my ability to blend. It also played to the strength that I knew the station like the back of my hand; I hoped my assassin had ever been.

My plan to track and subdue the assassin depended solely on how much information he had about the operation. Would he know that the drop was a security locker on the outer ring of the stations central core? The locker terminal was close to Adair's Pub and across the way from several small apartments. The nice thing about the small apartments, with their views of the expansive cylindrical city in space and the spires that rose along the central core, was that they also looked down on the street near the lockers.

The station had been built as a large cylinder, with multiple levels and multiple rings flowing out from the central spire that housed the transport system. The first ten levels of the station were docking bays, warehouses and repair facilities. From there down, every level housed a varying array of apartments, shops, restaurants and anything the weary traveler might need.

I knew that tracking and subduing a professional assassin was a difficult proposition on a good day, but I needed to do it. Timing and resources would be critical. Haelstrom was over a mile long, housing hundreds of thousands of people who were mostly transients or took up permanent residence on the station. It wasn't hard to imagine that a person could get lost on the station, or lose themselves on the station. As space stations went throughout the colonized Republic sphere of influence, Haelstrom was the largest and most active.

The first piece of the plan involved the locker, and the second involved the apartment that went along with the locker. The level and ring where the locker and apartment were located seemed fairly deserted, considering the time I arrived; station night was what they called it, based on local Drandeloin time, I'd arrived in the middle of the night. It was a chance I had to take. Had I beat him to the station?

The locker held the keycard to a cleaned apartment, smuggled self-defense hardware and whatever mission details needed to be passed. In his haste to strip the computer, the assassin hadn't grabbed my handler's drop keys, which I recovered among other items before blowing up the apartment. His disinterest in random items, or his lack of knowledge of how the system worked, gave me an advantage. I could watch and bait the locker.

Making certain I wasn't being followed, I slipped into the apartment, which hadn't been used in several months. The musty scent of dust and recycled air filled the room. The state of the room confirmed that I had the upper hand, at least for now.

I first set up a surveillance system in the window overlooking the "street." A small camera connected to a data recorder perched on the window gave me constant coverage of the locker and surrounding areas. I had no illusions that picking this needle in a haystack would be difficult, but such was life.

Once confident everything was in its place to watch for the assassin, I gathered up what items I didn't need for the short term or couldn't carry on me. I had rented a second apartment, up two levels and across the station, for me to hole up. My first run-in with the assassin reminded me that despite the fact that it was a "safe house," the life of a spy is always filled with intrigue.

Try as I might, I hadn't been able to pinpoint an occurrence in the past months where any of this started. Of course, one downside of working as independent units was that we didn't have regular board meetings to keep everyone abreast of the latest compromise or unexpected death of a team. There was net chatter between teams and the occasional tie together for big missions, but the whole network going silent in less than a month seemed rather disturbing. I didn't know the real number of active units; I had my suspicions, and if correct, it would bother me even more if they were all gone.

Three days of monitoring the locker, both from a distance and from my remote camera, began to look futile. As the hours dragged on, I wondered if the steady flow of different faces meant that I was barking up the wrong tree.

As I contemplated the possibility that the plan was falling apart, I caught sight of a familiar face; someone who'd come by the locker a few times. In a station with this many people, the chances of seeing someone multiple times in the same place were slim. The particular interest he gave to the lockers and the area around the lockers on multiple occasions stood out as a reasonable flag.

He picked a seat at a nearby café with a view on the locker; a spot he could observe discreetly for a few hours. He wasn't a memorable sort. Light brown skin, a long oval face with an equally long skinny nose. His curly black hair was cut short, a matching short beard cut above his jawbone faded into his cheeks. His dark green oval eyes scanned the faces. His dark blue hip-length sleeveless buckled coat hung open, revealing a hard muscular torso under a tight gray shirt. A slight bulge in the left side of his coat suggested a side holster of some sort. While he carried no obvious weapons, it wasn't hard to imagine he had one or more hidden somewhere.

The caliber of the station's security measures meant he had to rely on non-projectile or energy weapons within the station, unless he was able to smuggle or buy on the black market. While not impossible, the former would be hard, unless he was well connected. The latter would be expensive enough, and hopefully out of his profit margin. My one advantage was the support package set up for operatives on Haelstrom, support that would likely end with me provided me with reliable weapons.

The heavy flow of traffic down the corridor allowed me to move undetected from my perch. I had to make my approach look credible. Ensuring I didn't look in his direction, I searched the area for a minute, scanning the faces carefully. Reaching the locker, I used the swipe card to open it, then I removed the contents I had replaced the day I arrived. I pretended to ruffle through the contents before I closed the door and walked away.

As I travelled along the long corridors, pretending to browse the multitude of shops and vendors, I used reflective surfaces to keep an eye out for any signs of pursuit. He caught me by surprise as I saw the reflection of him only a few feet behind me, the thin matte black knife showing in his hand. Tension took over as I realized that I was cornered. I began reaching for the pistol I carried inside my coat when I realized he was gone. He was good, I couldn't deny that, but why had he vanished all of a sudden?

Staying to the busy areas of the station, I moved away as quickly as I could, keeping a wary eye out for any sign of him. Using the opening to work out the rest of my plan, I stopped at an interweb café, hoping to force the original buyers of the Cypher to move. I used the original thread set up for the first sale.

Crystal Goddess – Been traveling a while but finally passing through Haelstrom, thought we could meet for kava. Meet you at the Brown Five Dive when you're free. Hope you like shiny things. It's your turn to pay the tab this time! - Blackknight

I figured those who wanted the Cypher were watching, it wouldn't take them long to figure out where I wanted them; then it was a matter of how long till they joined us. I'd left the details vague on purpose to force them to set a time and date. The part of the station I suggested was not a place people just wandered through.

As I waited for my trace crystal to scramble the activity on the terminal, I used the reflective surfaces to look for a sign of him. The last thing I needed was him knowing I knew of him. As long as he thought he controlled the board, I was free to move.

I finally caught sight of him as I was leaving the café. Not wanting another close call, I wandered into the local casino, where the open floorplan and security could keep him at bay. Meandering through the various groupings of tables and throngs of people, I gravitated toward the high-risk games. Being good at most forms of gambling, I tended to favor Thrones and Ka Lon.

Thrones was a great way to spend hours fleecing other men out of their money, but Ka Lon was high stakes and chance. Two things I needed.

Typically a game designed to suck the savings out of your average travelers, Ka Lon required the smart gambler to observe the table and understand where the table was trending. A lot of the decisions came from both the cards active on the table and the sequence of the dice rolls. More than just a matter of luck or random chance, strategy and planning were involved, as well.

The assassin took up a perch on a far wall, where he could keep an eye on me. A mirrored pillar behind the table across from me gave me an unobstructed view.

As the dealer started the next hand, I ordered a black martini with a twist of narange, a local Drandelion fruit, from a roaming waitress and considered the four men and two women at the table with me. Usually searching for tells or signals, my senses were heightened even more as I searched for the assassin.

I guessed that two of the men and the women were together by, the way they talked and hung on each other. They wore sport coats and slacks, and skimpy form-fitting dresses. Their demeanor was relaxed and friendly which I read as tourists here for the fun side of Haelstrom.

The other two men were more likely here on business, passing through with an opportunity to stop at the casino. The gruff face of one man led me to assume that he either had a hard day of meetings or hard luck at the table. The lack of chips in front of him had me leaning toward the latter, but either way, he wasn't having a good day.

The other man's laissez faire attitude about the whole game seemed like a bad sign to me; men who had nothing to lose were not men I wanted to gamble against.

I played through a few small hands, trying to get a feel for the table. Not long after my fourth less-than-amazing hand and two very strong drinks, a woman stepped up to the table, seemingly watching the game and deciding if she wanted to join in. She was taller than me, and long raven hair framed her soft angular face. Her athletic figure was tightly bound up in a violet bodysuit. The leather top was zipped halfway down her full chest, and it seemed to strain to contain its fleshy contents.

There was something so dangerous and alluring about her. I found my eyes drifting to her, no matter how I tried to avoid it. Eventually, our eyes locked, then a twisted smirk pulled one side of her cheek and lips up before she broke eye contact.

There was something intimidating about that smile, but I let the feeling go as I realized that this was one of those rare women who were immune to my natural charms.

My thoughts and attention slid back to the game, and without reason, I realized that the mysterious woman had vanished. I hadn't seen her leave, but then my thoughts had pulled me out of reality for a moment.

Not feeling any real energy at the table, I waited for the latest hand to end, then I cashed out and headed for the door. It suddenly occurred to me that I'd lost focus on the assassin. A quick search of the area where I'd last seen him came up empty.

Cursing myself for losing contact with a man determined to kill me, realizing that the toll of the past few weeks was starting to have an effect on my focus, I fixed my mildly intoxicated mind on safety. The safe apartment I'd rented wasn't far from the casino; perhaps subconsciously I'd done that on purpose, but right now I was thankful for the short walk.

****

I was having a lovely dream about a pair of gorgeous beauties getting ready to inflict all sorts of adult-orientated pleasures upon my more-than-willing self. I smiled with the deep contentment of a man who doesn't care if he's dreaming, as long as he dies before the dream ends.

"Oh, Rah," Beauty one began, her warm hands caressing me in many places, "I can't wait to buzz your buzz..."

"What the BUZZ?" I questioned, frowning. Then Beauty One turned to Beauty Two, a look of confusion on her face.

"Buzz- Buzz - Buzz," she asked the second who responded with an equally quizzical "Buzz buzz- buzz - BUZZ!"

I was pulled rather brusquely from the delicious depths of the deepest slumber, a pharmaceutical-induced heaven, and dragged back into the reality of a dimly lit room. A Promium-and-vodka-induced hangover pounded through my head almost as boisterously as the asshole assailing my door. A faint whiff of something strange that smelled like cheese filled my mind. I groaned. The buzzing continued.

I reached to the nightstand next to the bed for the RendarCorp GX55 High Yield Slug thrower. With the instrument of mass destruction in my hand, I growled in frustration and aimed it at the incessant buzzing coming from behind the door. For a brief moment, I considered firing, but then wisdom caught up with the hangover and I decided against it.

For one thing, I had to admit that I have an unnerving and disgusting respect for human life, and for another, the GX55 was anything but silent. The last thing my headache needed at this moment was the thundering detonation of my hand-sized cannon. Instead, I rolled to the side of the bed and vomited.

43

As I wretched my guts on the floor, the fog in my head dissipated, bringing me back to the reality of my situation. It was reasonable that the person assailing my door was not the assassin. Why announce himself in this way? Who even knew I was here?

Questions raced through my pounding head as I rose with difficulty, groping for something to wear. I clamored my way into my dress pants from earlier in the evening, slipping the GX55 into the waistband along my back; I stepped up and opened the door.

As the door slid open, the error of my action came crashing through my mind. First, I'd opened myself to whatever was outside the door without regard to my current situation. Second, I'd put the gun in my waistband. Had I a moment to consider the situation, I might have taken said moment to blame my still drunken disoriented state of mind.

The real irony of that moment was that as the door opened and I caught my first glimpse of her, time seemed to slow. Her raven black hair, strong predatory eyes, full purplish lips and athletic frame bundled up in a tight-fitting violet body suit held me frozen in time for a split second.

Had it been anyone else – the assassin for instance – my reflexes and instincts might have kicked in with an unnerving drive for self-preservation, forcing me to pull the gun from my waistband. But something about this woman held me like a planet caught in the undeniable gravity of a failing star. It wasn't until the hooked twist to her grin and she lunged toward me that I realized how royally fragged I was.

My instincts and reflexes overcame my mesmerized mind just in time to move as her lunge reached me. All I really succeeded in doing, however, was to throw both of us off balance as we tumbled into the room. I bounced off the bed and she rolled over me, landing hard on the floor.

Still somewhat upright as I caught myself on the mattress, I turned to her with a smug look of superiority at her failed attempt to capture me. My grin vanished as quickly as it appeared when her athletic legs swept my feet out from under me. I dropped hard on my back against the corner of the bed.

Landing with a thud, the instant it took me to refocus, she was barreling into me from the side. Face down on the floor with me underneath her, I groaned, "This is awkward." Then, with a push off the floor, I used the momentum to land an elbow onto the side of her head. Rolling with her, I pinned her against the frame of the bed.

Before I knew it, she had my arm pulled up over my head, her hands were trying to lock behind my neck. Throwing my head back, I smashed it against her head, and was rewarded with a feminine yelp. Her arm went slack for a moment, giving me room to roll away.

Attempting to scramble to my feet, a sudden stunning flash appeared before my eyes as a striking pain shot through my head. I pitched forward, having not gained my balance, I found myself once again on the floor. A second later, the weight of my assailant and the click of my GX55 registered before the stars in my eyes cleared.

The funny thing about my current predicament was that I found her even more alluring sitting on top of me, having captured me with my own gun.

"I would say something witty and humorous at this point, but I don't get the feeling you're the charmable type."

For a long moment, she leered down the barrel of my gun at me like a cat that had cornered its prey. Without so much as a word, she dropped the gun to the side, and pulled me up into a long lusty kiss. My mind reeled at the sudden change of events, until I realized I'd been unconsciously pumping pheromones into the room as we wrestled.

Don't get me wrong, I'm not one to balk when an attractive, skilled woman kisses me all of a sudden, but you have to understand my surprise.

Our lustful kiss swiftly turned into a flurry of wild hands groping at various areas of each other's body. At some point, the zipper to her body suit came undone, as did the belt and button on my slacks. The curious thing about my current drunken state, with a room full of pheromones, was how everything beyond that point turned to a blur of flesh, moans and sweat.

When the world started making sense again, we were both lying on the floor not far from where we had begun. Still panting, we silently stared up at the ceiling.

"I don't suppose this was part of your plan?" I asked.

"You could say that!" she responded fighting to catch her breath.

"What did they tell you about me?"

"You were some sort of thief. Corporate espionage spook."

"Am I supposed to be dead or alive?" I kept the conversation going, knowing my talent was affecting her judgment. I wasn't one to take advantage of a vulnerable woman, but at this moment, I was just as vulnerable.

"Honestly, the contract is to retrieve the cube. Fetching you is a bonus."

Her answer struck me as curious. It wasn't likely the original buyers had responded this soon. On the other hand, it was obvious she wasn't working for the assassin, or I would have been dead a long time ago. I was losing count of the people involved in this puzzle.

"And where were you supposed to deliver yours truly and the Cypher, once we were under your spell?" I asked

"Kellis IV. At least, that's where they wanted the cube. The contract didn't specify where to deliver you. I just assumed they wanted their tech returned and the guy who stole it captured."

I couldn't help but raise an eyebrow at her comment. My mind mulled the new data, and then I pulled myself up. I propped myself up on my elbow and gazed at her taught athletic body; the rise and fall of her full breasts. Having availed myself of her body for however long we'd been naked on the floor, my mind was more able to focus on the data and less on the full mounds before them. I mentally ran through the list of Drandelion corporations in or around the Kellis system. A handful came to mind, but that didn't mean someone with influence over one of those corporations wasn't pulling the strings.

"Ok, I have to ask...." My curiosity was killing me, and I was sure that the change in the tone of my voice translated this well. "How did you find me?"

The mysterious bounty hunter did something else I hadn't expected. She giggled like a teenage girl. "You know you're being followed by a contract killer?"

While the news of the assassin was anything but a surprise, the simple fact that she knew about him and was using him to get to me seemed uncanny at best.

"Uh, yes, of course. I was trying to set a trap for him so I could get answers."

After a long minute, she turned to face me. She sat up against the foot of the bed as I continued to prop myself up on my arm, looking up at her. "I've been tracking him since I lost you on Talmeria. You dropped off the grid, but he kept searching for you. I figured he'd track you down eventually."

Her matter-of-fact revelation made me grin as I reflected how I never would have thought of that. "So what now?" I asked as if deep down inside I wanted her to reconsider her contract.

"I suppose it's up to you." She stared at me for a moment, those beautiful eyes glittering as she lost herself in thought. "On the one hand, you're cute, and to tell you the truth, I'm tired of tracking your ass across the Republic. On the other hand, while this contract is quickly becoming more expensive than it's worth, the bonus for you may balance out the trouble."

"Well…" I grinned back at her mischievously. "If you've been watching this assassin since Talmeria, you know him pretty well. You could help me figure this puzzle out, and with you watching my back, the payment we get for the Cypher should be worth more than whatever they're paying you to retrieve it."

If there was one sure thing about the corporate espionage black market on tech, it was that it would be easier and cheaper for a company to pay someone to steal a piece of stolen techthan it would be to buy it from the person who stole it, regardless of whether the company was the one that originally owned the tech,.

"Sounds like fun!" she said, a twinkle in her big beautiful eyes. "I can live with that, and if I get bored, I can always turn you in for the contract," she said with a wink.

I laughed, attempting to hide any uncertainty I had that she might actually follow through on the point.

"Fair enough," I said a bit surprised by her response, but willing to take advantage of it. "Call me Rah. But I'm sure you already knew my name." I extended a hand. A shake seemed rather unnecessary, considering what we'd just done, but I thought, polite is polite.

"Violet Black," she responded, taking my hand with a firm grip. "And no, I didn't already know your name. Details on your identity are sketchy at best. It's nice to meet you, Rah."

****

Violet's knowledge of our would-be assassin turned out to be better than I had estimated. While she knew nothing about who was doing this or why, she knew enough about how he operated to put us in a position to act rather than simply react. Violet worked out an intricate plan to offer a couple of prime opportunities to end the mission, only to block him at the last minute. Working on the premise that if we frustrated him enough and at the right times, that he'd lose focus and allow us to turn the tables on him, capturing him before he could react. While the overall premise seemed sound, I feared the time constraints we would have in pushing him to the edge before the actual Cypher drop took place.

The buyers agreed to my location and asked for forty-eight hours, so we had less than two days to corner and question the assassin. I was just glad I didn't need to use the drop as a way to corner him. She was the perfect blocker, putting random people in his path with bumps just long enough to lose sight of me, or closing a door to slow or stop his progress before he could get close enough to strike.

"I think he's ready!" she said with a grin.

"I hope so. I'm tiring of this game."

We both watched him from an upper catwalk that looked down on one of the merchant streets. We'd been careful to weave our way into the less desirable regions of the station, intending to corner him and lock him down until we could get the information we wanted.

"You go get in position. I'll lead him down there."

I finished as I gave Violet a nod. She returned the look with a witty smile and a wink. As she walked away, I turned and looked down over the catwalk one last time before I headed for the stairs. He was ducking in and out of shops, trying to figure out which one I had disappeared into, which meant I had to time it right.

I slipped up alongside a group of three people walking between my target and me long enough to get up to a store he hadn't reached yet, to put a significant distance between us. Once out in the open, I had to use my skill and my surroundings to keep him close enough so I didn't lose sight of him, but kept far enough away that I didn't leave myself open. Without Violet running interference until we hit the last corridor, it would have been hard to lead him on without him realizing the game.

I slipped into a deserted engineering section, which was a maze of doors that led to large rooms filled with all sorts of machinery. The heat and noise levels, plus the random clouds of steam or smoke, made this place an assassin's wet dream.

It was also the perfect place to use these elements against him.

At this point, I wondered if he had sensed a trap the way I had when we first crossed paths, or if he was completely blind at this point to the implications of this chase.

Down one more corridor – this one filled with monitoring equipment – and he'd be far enough off of the beaten path that I assumed he'd be suspicious enough to strike. His footsteps got louder, and I turned just in time to catch the violet blur that was my cohort barrel into the man from the side.

The clamor of metal tools and equipment falling to the floor filled the corridor as they both crashed into a box of equipment. He pushed her off, throwing a nearby pipe. Violet backpedaled. As soon as he pushed her away, he lunged toward me with a matte black knife in his hand. She spun, throwing a foot into the back of his leg as he moved towards me. Her strike threw him off balance as he barreled over in my direction.

I spun off to the side, keeping his knife hand away from my body, then pushed him in a perpendicular direction as he fell headlong past me. My push altered his balance, and he crashed into a console of monitors.

Violet was there as he recovered. He swung the knife, she parried with her arm. He made a pointed thrust at her, but Violet's hand caught his arm just behind his knife hand. She carried his momentum and pulled him forward as her arm slammed into his jaw.

He swept his leg up under hers, throwing off her balance. Violet's grip dropped from his knife hand as she fell. He staggered back from the hit as she dropped to the floor, rolling up between him and me.

"Stop!" I yelled as I pulled the GX55 from my coat. Leveling the gun at him I hoped he was a smarter assassin than I was a shot. Don't get me wrong, I can shoot when I need to, but I'm just as likely to shoot him in the leg as the head.

He stopped for a moment as Violet moved to my left. Keeping a clear field of fire, she moved closer to him while staying between us. The devious grin that crossed the man's rather plain face was unexpected and puzzling. At least until the small disk he threw down at the floor exploded at his feet. The air between us filled instantly with a heavy white smoke, random bolts of electricity shot in every direction from the blast point.

"Marvin, watch him!" Violet yelled as she inched toward the cloud and lightning.

"I can't see him!" I yelled back, uncertain if she'd been talking to me.

"Never mind," she said, looking back as she sprinted forward through the cloud. Since there was no indication of any harm coming to her after she disappeared into the smoke, I followed.

"Do I want to know?" I asked, catching up to her from behind as she charged headlong down the corridor. The only answer I received was a devilish grin as her eyes focused on our assailant.

I may have mentioned earlier that this was a maze of rooms, storage spaces and engineering equipment. The assassin took to the ever-changing environment much like a rat trying to evade a cat. He ducked through doors, jumped over boxes and equipment, and threw random objects into our path in an attempt to slow us down.

The gleam in Violet's eyes and her laser focus on the assassin as he moved in and out of our view drew a shudder along my spine. We'd spent the better part of the almost two days together since she barged into my room, but I still hadn't been able to find out much about her. From what I'd seen, though, she was a superbly focused bounty hunter whose mind was as sharp and capable as her body.

The assassin upended a box of parts as he ran by. The multiple metal pieces flew in every direction as Violet tracked his every move. She weaved her way through the scattered collection of parts with the grace of a cat. Grabbing a large boxy part a little bigger than her hand, she heaved it underhanded like a projectile as they ran.

Crashing down against the floor at the man's feet, the part she threw caused him to trip, losing his balance just as he came to the edge of a corridor which led to a public street. Violet rammed into him at full speed. They both collided through people and displays. Screams of surprise and confusion, mixed with a healthy dose of flying paper and other random products, combined to form utter chaos as I followed closely behind.

The commotion drew my attention, but not for so long that I didn't catch the assassin running down the corridor to my left.

"Go!" Violet yelled at me as I started toward her to offer assistance as she attempted to extricate herself from a pile of displays and debris. I turned after him, running as hard as I could to keep him in sight. We were running through a public street now, dodging people and tables and displays every so often.

He did what he could to push people in my way, or upturn tables and displays in my way to slow me down. I had to admit that my speed wasn't equal to his, but his attempts to slow my progress worked against him, slowing him down with each movement.

He turned down another side corridor. Not certain Violet was behind me or what had happened to her, I kept up the pace so I could keep him in my sights. I knew that if I lost track of him this time, our little game of cat and mouse that had spanned Republic space would likely be punctuated by a high velocity bullet to the skull.

I noticed the end of the corridor was approaching quickly, opening up to one of the station's maintenance gangways that they used to service the core of the station's heavy equipment.

"Stop!" I yelled, pulling the GX55 out of my coat, slowing my progress to get a better bearing on him. My breath was ragged and my pulse raced, forcing me to concentrate on his movement toward the end of the corridor. Gunfire echoed down the corridor, then he spun around violently, throwing his balance off just as a blur of something hit him from the side of the corridor.

As I reached the end of the hallway, Violet staggered back across the gangway. Before I knew it, a metal pipe smashed into my hand, knocking the gun away. Pain tore through my arm, causing me to kneel to maintain my balance. I looked up just in time to see the assassin standing over me with the metal pipe over his head, pausing only for a moment before he began a downward blow. Time slowed as my wounded arm came up in my defense.

Halfway through his attack, something pulled him backwards, throwing him into a spin. He slammed into the metal rail, turning just in time to swing at Violet as she approached. She jumped back out of the way of the pipe.

He stepped forward, swinging again with a side arm attack. He used his upper torso to throw his weight into the blow, but Violet ducked just in time, dropping down and holding herself off the ground with just her hand in a very feline acrobatic move. As he swung past her, she shifted her weight and kicked, driving the assassin back toward the rail.

"No!" I yelled as I watched him roll over the rail, the metal pipe banging its way along the machinery below.

Violet and I arrived at the rail together, to find him hanging precariously by both hands from a support beam under the main walkway.

"Give me your hand!" I yelled down to him as he dangled just a few inches beyond my reach.

"You've gotta be crazy!" he responded. "Either way I'm dead!"

"Give me your hand and you have my word that we will let you go once you tell me what this is all about!"

He grinned, and that look didn't bode well for my plans. "Even if I let you save me, I failed my mission!" he yelled over the sound of machinery. "There is nothing left for me!"

"I'll vanish, and you can say you killed me. Say you completed your mission. I don't care, as long as you stop chasing me and I find out why you were sent!"

His hands were starting to slip. "It doesn't work like that, Rah. You know how things work as well as I do."

At that moment, a serene look fell across his face. A second later, his hands slipped from the rail. The serene look on his face continued as he fell, right up to the point where he smashed headlong into a large obtrusive series of station engineering systems below.

Violet and I stared at his broken body as it hung on the edge of one of the machines. I had hoped I'd feel a sense of finality or satisfaction upon seeing the man who murdered my handler, among so many others, meet his doom. Instead, the only thing I felt was a heavy pit in my stomach at the loss of a chance to find answers to a whole host of lingering questions.

"Violence, my dear..." I paused, considering the sudden impromptu nickname. A smile stretched across my face as I realized there would need to be a small level of control placed on Violet if we were going to work together. "...it works better if we interrogate the baddies before we throw them off a bridge."

"Make sure you tell the baddies that the next time they're trying to smash you with a metal pipe," she responded with a sly grin.

"Touché," I said, giving her a dramatic bow.

"Would telling you that I know where he was staying matter now?" she asked.

My head jerked, to catch her eyes. She grinned bigger as our eyes met. All I could do was shake my head and smile as I walked back to retrieve my gun.

****

"Marvin, open sesame."

The card she pulled from the back of the small handheld device went into the key slot, but the real trick was how talking to her little device

52

convinced the door to open without so much as an alarm or protest. Being a standard small apartment: bed, bathroom, kitchenette and a small table with a couple of chairs, there wasn't much to search. By the state of the room, it looked as if he hadn't done much besides sleep there in the few days he had been on the station.

"I don't suppose I need to tell you where to look. He's a trained operator."

Violet nodded as I offered guidance. The futility of this search was not lost on me. I understood that he could have been carrying all of his information on a crystal, or had it locked away somewhere that only he could find or access. I took heart in the fact that he'd had little time to prepare his hunting grounds prior to catching sight of me, so I hoped it was possible he hadn't had time to hide.

After three hours, we had essentially torn the living space apart searching. Violet sat across the small round table from me as we stared down at the three small items we'd found in the room that were not part of the original decor: a data crystal, a credit chip and a Republic Ident card which we both assumed had to be fake.

"Well?" Violet asked, looking up from the items to me.

"Unfortunately, we don't have time to pursue this," I responded, grabbing the three items. "I have a drop I need to meet in two hours, and we still need to prep the field."

"You want me on the ground with you or observing?" She inquired.

"I promised this time I'd be alone. But I'd appreciate the overwatch."

I realized there was a chance that this whole situation was a way to bring the Cypher out into the open so she could retrieve it. Still, the truth of the situation was that my instincts told me she was exactly what she came across as: a strong-willed bounty hunter with a penchant for violence and a drive to support her own enlightened self-interest.

We didn't bother putting the room back the way we found it. Eventually, the owners would find him and realize they'd lost their rent along with any recovery of damages. His fate couldn't be helped, and neither could the state of the room.

Locking the door behind us, I led Violet through the station to the locker I had stashed my gear in. Pulling a small black bag out, I checked the contents. The Cypher remained exactly where I left it, wrapped up in a black velvet bag on the bottom of the pack. Pulling an autoinjector and a vial of Promium from the bag, I inserted the vial into the injector and applied the tip to the skin under the waist of my pants. With a soft hiss, the vial emptied into my body.

"What's that?" she inquired as she watched me.

"Promium. I have a condition that requires regular injections." I fed her a deliberately vague answer, realizing that giving her too much personal information too soon might be dangerous. I hadn't made it as long as I had in this job by being careless or letting my guard down, no matter how attractive and alluring the reason.

"Damn, I wish someone had told me about that," she replied with her usual mischievous grin. "It would have been much easier to track you."

"There's a reason no one thought to use that to track me" I said with a wink. The reason of course was that no matter how deep the compromise of our network went, the intimate details of the program that had altered me were buried somewhere deep in a Republic archive under some obscure codename only the people in charge of the program remembered. As far as anyone knew, I was a ghost and only maybe a handful of people in the whole galaxy knew my real identity.

"Of course," she responded, then started laughing.

****

"Did you bring it?" the tall muscular man asked as we stood across from each other, a small crate filling the space between us. I recognized the man from the original drop. He'd been the lead man who'd taken the spray of blood from the unfortunate woman who took my bullet. Neither his demeanor nor his wardrobe had changed much since the last time we crossed paths.

His face still looked way too serious, and his suit was tailored and dark like so many private security forces I'd run into over the years.

"Of course. Do you have my creds?"

"Forty thousand," he said, pulling a credit chip from his inner coat pocket.

"You know I can't be sure, but according to the late Mr. Hood, it's not complete." I baited the hook, watching his face.

"Who?" he asked, his face barely changing.

"Mr. Hood. You know, the portly gentleman your soldiers killed on Taldera a few weeks ago. The last time I tried to sell the cube."

Now it was my turn to be surprised as his face barely flinched. Either he was a very good operative who could hide his emotions well, or he really had no idea what I was talking about.

"The last time we were supposed to meet on Talmeria, someone started taking potshots at my men." He replied with very little change in his expression.

"An unfortunate misunderstanding," I said with a smile. "As it turns out, there have been a number of factions working to retrieve this, along with me."

The man simply nodded.

I placed the cube on the small crate, sitting softly on top of the felt bag I'd been carrying it in. The man set the credit chip down on the table. I picked up the chip, scanning it with a handheld reader, standard issue for this type of transaction. The standard reader simply checked the balance on the credit chip. Mine had been modified a few years ago by a trusted asset into a skimmer to pull the credits from the card and transfer them during a drop to avoid any "trust issues." After the credits were collected, they followed the same parameters as all my personal accounts, moving around a lot out of the view of my previous benefactors.

Once the reader confirmed the transactions had been completed, I looked up at the man. "Pleasure finally doing business with you," I said with a nod. "If you're ever in need of my services, please don't hesitate to contact me. I promise to keep the weapons fire out of it."

The man's face shifted slightly, the most incomprehensible smile curling the edges of his mouth as he picked up the Cypher, placed it in the bag, and turned to leave. I waited until he was well out of sight before turning back toward where Violet was perched. As I walked through the door at the other end of the room, Violet jumped down from a stack of boxes to land directly beside me.

"Well? That seemed to go smoothly enough." She commented.

I nodded. "Oddly enough, yes. I rather expected something different to happen, but I am happy that damnable thing is out of my hands now."

After a moment, she said, "And they didn't try to swindle you. That's curious."

"Nope, I'm not complaining. I'll transfer the amount to your account as soon as you give it to me."

"Don't bother. We're going to need all the credits we can get our hands on if we're going off the grid." She replied.

I was dumbfounded by the response. I had been happy to pay her off for helping me and not collecting on my head. My overpowering instinct toward self-preservation drove that train, but her suggestion that we would need the funds together was an exciting prospect I had never imagined.

****

We spent the next week digging through the data trail connected to the items we'd found in the assassin's apartment. The credit chip had been a payment for expenses and his job so far, minus the success of liquidating me. The origination point of the credits on the chip met a relative dead end being an unassociated account located in a Republic bank. It was a trail we could follow, but I didn't expect it to go any further.

As I suspected, the identity card had been a fake, but the quality and the level of detail involved in creating an ID like that and associating it with an established cover identity told me that the creator of the card was well placed, well financed and well connected, either in Megacorp or Republic circles. Either way, all it told me was that whoever had ordered the eradication of an entire corporate espionage unit had a lot of power and play.

Then, there was the final piece, the data crystal. Our would-be assassin could now be credited with over one hundred and twenty kills. Based on the information we found in the crystal, the operation had been limited to one assassin. I found it hard to believe that one man was responsible for the death of so many trained operatives, but there it was.

In an effort to keep operational control and secrecy to a minimal level, whoever put the plan in place wanted it to happen slowly, with a minimum of warning to the teams. By my estimation of the data he had available on all of the teams and their missions at the time, there were less than a handful of teams still active, and from the activity on the usual communications channels, all had gone silent.

We were still no closer to solving the problem than we were before, except we knew there were others out there who were in the same boat I was. It wasn't much, but it was a direction.

"Where to now?" Violet asked me with a playful quip to her voice.

"Dunno, love. Maybe we can track one of these other fellows down and get some answers." I grinned at my new partner. "Either way, it should be fun!"

EPILOGUE

Rah's thoughts were on Kelvis' message as he walked along the corridor to the target's room. *Why now?* He thought the timing was the most curious part of the whole equation. Could he have just uncovered it, or had it simply taken Kelvis this long to track him down? This had been the closest Rah had been to Republic space in two years. *How could Kelvis have known they could get to Freeport 5 in time?*

As Rah came around the corner, he hesitated.

"Vi, we have a problem," he whispered to the food tray.. "There are two guards, not one!"

Resolved to not let the plan go awry, Rah pushed forward. With only a moment of concentration, he told his body to start secreting pheromones that would cause confusion. One of the advantages of being a burned operative, genetically manipulated to serve a function, was that if they didn't kill an agent when they burned him, they can't take away his skills.

Rah had never been too sure what they did to him, as much of his memory prior to the procedure was missing. They wanted an operative who could talk his way through corporate espionage rather than fight his way in. Leaving his targets unaware of anything that might have happened tended to keep retaliations low.

Both efficient and effective at his job, figuring out how to manipulate different pheromones to create different effects let Rah woo women and put men off their guard. He wondered if the organization who he'd worked for considered how dangerous Rah coupled with an operative with a penchant for violence might be.

An invisible cloud of chemicals floated around Rah as he approached the end of the hall. The goal, behind door number two, was prime for the taking, but blocked by the two seated men, who looked like holovid wrestlers. As a rule, Rah would have no doubts about Violet's ability to subdue even the largest threat, but he started to wonder as he looked them up and down.

Both men stood as he approached, one stood closer to Rah than the other guard, who stayed closer to the door. It dawned on Rah that the way the men staggered their position gave the one farther back a clear field of fire.

"Good morning, gentlemen. I have breakfast for 913." The first guard looked at Rah, then back to his companion, both of their brows furrowed with uncertainty. The ex-spy knew the chemicals would take a moment to affect them, so he simply waited with a patient smile on his face.

"We didn't order any breakfast." He noticed the familiar glaze fill their eyes as the chemical hit their brain.

"Well, of course, you didn't. The guest in 913 did. I have the bill right here."

He held up a small black bi-fold. Both men stepped closer, their minds foggy with Rah's suggestion of an order the foremost thing on their mind. Both men stepped up to the cart, the guard farther away forgetting his training as they flanked the right and left sides of the cart, leaving the front of the cart open to the door.

"Excuse me!" Violet, suddenly standing at the end of the cart with a spray can in each hand, the nozzles pointed at the guards. Both men turned toward Violet as distorted reasoning showed on their faces. A cloud of gas filled the air before them as it sprayed from each can into their faces. Within seconds, they dropped to the floor with resounding thumps

"Nice!" Rah exclaimed as he pulled two small cylinders from under the cart. He handed one to Violet, then moved with familiar efficiency toward the two doors that flanked the center door. They pulled cover tape off the sticky strips and placed the canisters at the bottom frame of each door. A thin wire tied to the door handle ensured the canister would trip when the door opened.

With a smile, Violet stood and moved to the target door, pulling a black handgun from a shoulder holster. Rah stepped up to the frame side of the door with the key card. With a nod from Violet, Rah slid the key card into the slot and waited for the green bulb at the top of the lock to illuminate.

A long moment passed as they both watched, realizing the key was not going to unlock the door.

"Are you kidding me?" His head shaking. "And this was going so well."

Rah slid the key into the slot once more. With no difference in outcome, rolling his eyes in frustration he pulled the key out.

"Vi, my love. Please!" Rah implored with a welcoming gesture. Rah pulled his gun and traded places with Violet as she inserted a small card in the slot and pulled out her small handheld computer.

"You know, this would be so much easier if I could just blow the door!" she said with a grin as she checked her computer. "Marvin, open sesame!" she said to the device.

A moment of silence passed until the small light on the keypad turned green and they heard a noticeable click. Violet returned the card and computer to a pocket of her jacket. She pulled her handgun back out before turning the knob and pushing in the door.

"Who the hell are you?" a rather obese man yelled at them as Rah and Violet burst into the room.

Violet quickly moved straight for the man as Rah closed the door and ensured the locking mechanism activated. The large man stood on the far side of the bed, his belly testing the limits of the rope that held his hotel robe closed. His thinning gray hair still showed signs of moisture from a shower. He had a long handlebar mustache that dipped down past the edges of his lips, and a sharply pointed goatee on his round chin.

"Guar—" He started as Violet grabbed him, a white rag pressed hard against his mouth. Rah moved over to the desk, where a silver briefcase sat. He expertly checked the locking mechanism.

She finished taping the large unconscious man to a chair he barely fit in.

"I don't suppose we have time to get the combination out of him," Violet mused.

Rah searched around the room to make sure there were no other decoy silver briefcases.

"I'd say that's a no. Let's go, Vi!" Rah grabbed the case as two loud bangs resonated through the hallway outside, shaking the walls and doors. Rah looked to Violet, and her devilish smile reminded him how he appreciated her attention to details as looked toward the balcony.

"Plan B!" she joked as she pulled a small rectangular transmitter from her inside coat pocket and pressed a button. A third explosion vibrated the door and walls as unintelligible yelling sounded from outside the door.

Violet pulled a small roll of gray cord from a pouch on her hip. Unrolling the soft pliable cord, she placed it in a circle in the middle of the floor.

"Gentex, really?" Rah quipped before stepping back against the wall.

Violet shot her uncertain companion a crafty look as she placed a small piece of metal with a blinking light on the edge of the cord and walked to the wall by Rah. On her small transmitter, she pressed a second button. A fourth bang filled the room, causing a large circle of dust to appear in the floor.

Violet stepped up to the hole and looked down at the plaster and ferrocrete now gathered rather untidily in the room beneath them. With an excited grin, Violet dropped into the hole and disappeared. Rah shook his head in disbelief and, after dropping the case first, followed suit.

They both assumed a very casual nature as they strolled through the hallway to the elevator. Rah concentrated on filling the air around them with a pheromone that meant to make people not take notice of them.

The duo emerged from the elevator stepping from the compartment and out on the ground floor, into a scene of chaos. Hotel personnel were running around, trying to calm guests and coordinate evacuation procedures. A security guard stood talking to someone who Rah guessed might be the manager of the hotel and a number of local constables.

Rah and Violet stayed with the crowd as the hotel personnel guided people out of the building. Once free of the throng of guests, Rah and Violet strolled to the parking lot and their newly acquired vehicle, ready for a quick getaway.

The burned spy looked over at his companion, and laughed internally at the mischievous grin she wore as she tossed the briefcase into the back seat.

Rah pulled away just as the Republic Crisis Response vehicles pulled into the driveway in front of the hotel.

"Subtle...very subtle, my dear!" Rah exclaimed as he drove, checking the rear cameras for any hint of pursuit.

"No one's dead, and there's nothing connecting us to the incident." They looked at each other, sharing a silent humorous moment of understanding, turning their focus to the drop.

"Transport leaves in four hours. We stop for a two-hour layover at Roermon station, where we'll meet the buyer and make the exchange. Then we catch a second transport to Freeport Five. I left the message for Kelvis last night. If everything goes well, it should be a quiet trip. Maybe now I can start getting some answers."

Violet nodded as they merged onto the highway and headed for the spaceport.

OPERATION: Mobius
The first full book in the Chronicles of Rah Series
Coming 14 Dec 2020

About the Author

Scott Hopkins is a budding author new to the science fiction scene. His hope is that his love of science fiction has finally brought him to the cusp of a very popular first full length novel and space opera series. He truly wishes to influence people through words and ideas and hopes to develop and share his visions of space and time with new readers.

As an avid reader of the classical sci-fi authors like William Gibson and Phillip K Dick, Douglas Adams and Orson Scott Card, he found a lot of expression and inspiration in the twisted plots of gritty otherworldly matters. While clean, utopian science fiction such as Star Trek has always been a good anchor for much inspiration, grittier sci-fi like Neuromancer and Blade Runner with their twisting plots and intrigue are the true field in which good sci-fi is cultivated and grown.

Other books by this author

Please visit your favorite ebook retailer to discover other
books by Scott Hopkins:

The Chronicles of Rah Series

Operation Mobius – Coming Soon

Mobius Strain – Coming soon

Connect with Scott Hopkins

I really appreciate you reading my book! Here are my
social media coordinates:

Friend me on Facebook:
https://www.facebook.com/ChronicleofRah/
Visit my website: https://www.ordernchaos.com

www.ingramcontent.com/pod-product-compliance
Lightning Source LLC
Chambersburg PA
CBHW032043180726
48284CB00008B/2733